"What 'great plan' did Hitler entrust you with?" Luke asked, turning to Gerda.

It was no use. Gerda Mueller was far away, swaying to some inner music.

"She's mad," Ms. Sheck said, but Luke wasn't so sure that she was. Not in the way that Ms. Sheck meant.

In a burst of understanding, it all came together. Luke had finally figured out the secret, hidden for more than a century, of the most boring book in the world.

Also by Brian Falkner

The Tomorrow Code
Brain Jack
The Assault

THE
PROJECT

BRIAN FALKNER

All rights reserved. Published in the United States by Ember, an imprint of Random House Children's Books, a division of Random House, Inc., New York. Originally published in paperback in Australia and New Zealand by Walker Books Australia, Newtown, in 2010, and subsequently published in hardcover in the United States by Random House Children's Books, New York, in 2011.

Ember and the E colophon are registered trademarks of Random House, Inc.

Visit us on the Web!
randomhouse.com/teens

Educators and librarians, for a variety of teaching tools,
visit us at randomhouse.com/teachers

The Library of Congress has cataloged the hardcover edition of this work as follows:
Falkner, Brian.
The project / Brian Falkner. — 1st ed.
p. cm.
Summary: After discovering a terrible secret hidden in the most boring book in the world, Iowa fifteen-year-olds Luke and Tommy find out that members of a secret Nazi organization intend to use this information to rewrite history.
ISBN 978-0-375-86945-7 (trade) — ISBN 978-0-375-96945-4 (lib. bdg.) —
ISBN 978-0-375-98350-4 (ebook)
[1. Time travel—Fiction. 2. Adventure and adventurers—Fiction. 3. Nazis—Fiction.
4. World War, 1939–1945—Germany—Fiction.] I. Title.
PZ7.F1947Pr 2011 [Fic]—dc22 2010033449

ISBN 978-0-375-87188-7 (trade pbk.)

RL: 4.7

Printed in the United States of America
10 9 8 7 6 5 4 3 2 1
First Ember Edition 2012

Random House Children's Books supports
the First Amendment and celebrates the right to read.

For Graham and Sue

CONTENTS

PART I: THE MOST BORING BOOK IN THE WORLD

Prologue   3

1. Busted   5
2. The Rain   15
3. Sandbags   17
4. Benfer   28
5. Dark Waters Rising   35
6. The Vitamin Man   47
7. Bad Moon   55
8. Dog-Face   63
9. Underwater   73
10. Black Friday   76

PART II: THE DETECTIVES

11. Godzilla the Squirrel   80
12. Vacation   84
13. The Library   87
14. A Lead   91
15. The Gift   96
16. Detective Work   98
17. The Briefcase   105
18. Memory   116
19. Werewolves   121

20. Just Walking   125

21. The Most Boring Book   128

22. The Vitruvian Men   132

23. Under Arrest   146

24. The Good/Bad Cop   154

PART III: **THE RIVER**

25. Children of the Wolves   164

26. The Lair   170

27. The Discovery   177

28. Princess   183

29. The Chamber   193

30. No Time   198

31. Forty-Four   205

32. Powerful Magic   216

33. Attacked   218

34. Goggles   222

35. Easy As   228

36. Devastation   230

37. A Fact   234

38. The Good Man   239

39. Corks   249

40. The Jaws of Death   254

41. The Mouth of Hell   260

Epilogue   273

PART I

THE MOST BORING BOOK IN THE WORLD

In rivers, the water that you touch is the last of what has passed and the first of that which comes; so with present time.
—Leonardo da Vinci

PROLOGUE

This is not the most boring book in the world.

This is a book *about* the most boring book in the world, which is a different book altogether.

This book is really interesting and exciting, and parts of it are quite funny.

The most boring book in the world, on the other hand, is really, really boring. It's a real clunker. It's so boring that if I told you what it was about, you'd be asleep before I got past the introduction. And so would I.

You might think that your history textbook is the most boring book in the world. But you are wrong. Or you might think that your auntie's book about dried flowers is the most boring book in the world, but that's like an action-packed adventure story compared to the *real* most boring book in the world.

The most boring book in the world is so boring that only one copy of it was ever printed. The story goes that the guy who was printing the book glanced down and started reading the pages as they were whizzing through the hand-turned press, and it was so boring that he fell asleep and knocked over a lantern onto a stack of paper, which caught fire and destroyed the printery. Only one copy survived. Which is probably a good thing.

The printer, whose name was Albert, was fired, but he found a cozy little job licking postage stamps at a post office in Moose Jaw, Canada, which sounds like the most boring job in the world, and it probably was, but he said it was still better than printing the most boring book in the world.

But this book is not about Albert. It's about the most boring book in the world. And, most of all, it is about me and Tommy, the ones who found the most boring book in the world, and the terrible things that took place after we found it.

1. BUSTED

"We would have got away with it if it wasn't for that drunken squirrel," said Luke. He managed a grin at Tommy, who was sitting next to him on the hard, slatted bench outside the vice principal's office.

As always, in the cold, hard light of the next day, their prank seemed childish and stupid. But this time, Luke had discovered the universal law of vice principals: Those in America had no better sense of humor than those back in New Zealand.

"Don't sweat it, dude," Tommy said. "I can handle Kerr."

"Yeah right."

Tommy's dad was a lawyer, and Tommy always thought he could talk his way out of anything. Sometimes he was right.

Tommy had a coin in his hand and was flipping it up in the air, catching it first on the top side of his fingers, then flipping his hand over and catching it on the underside.

"Seriously," he said. "I've been in more courtrooms than you've had hot dinners. I'm going to tie this sucker up in so many legal knots that he'll look like a . . . a . . . pretzel."

"Someone doing yoga," Luke said simultaneously.

"Yep, a pretzel doing yoga," Tommy said.

"I hope so."

"Just back me up on whatever I say."

"No worries about that, bro," Luke said.

Tommy flipped the coin a couple more times, then caught it in his palm and made a fist. "How many times?" he asked.

"How many times what?" Luke asked.

"How many times did I toss the coin? Get it right, you can keep the coin."

"Forty-seven," Luke said.

"You sure?"

"Yeah."

"How many of them were heads?" Tommy asked.

"Twenty-nine," Luke said.

"How many tails?"

"All the rest." Luke smiled.

Tommy flipped the coin to him. "That's freaky," he said. "How do you do that?"

"Dunno, bro."

It was true. He really didn't know. When he was younger, Luke had thought that everybody could remember things like he could and was surprised to find out that most people's memories were sieves. His memory was a blessing and a curse. In class he would scan the textbook at the start of the lesson and no longer need to concentrate. That led to hours of staring out of classroom windows or doodling in the margins of his workbooks. The boredom also led to some interesting pranks that were hilarious to him and his classmates but that, for some inexplicable reason, his teachers did not find funny.

The door to the office opened, and Ms. Sheck, their homeroom teacher, stood in the gap.

In her early twenties, she observed the strict dress code for teachers at the high school, with a simple skirt, a plain blouse, and sensible flat shoes. But she wore a bit too much eyeliner; there was a suspicious hole in the side of her nose; and her sprayed, clipped blond hair seemed to be struggling to bust out. If students were angry with Ms. Sheck, they called her Ms. Shrek, but she really didn't look anything like Shrek. Luke thought she looked more like Princess Fiona, the beautiful princess (in her non-ogre moments). All of the guys at the school thought she was really hot.

"Come in, boys," she said solemnly, but Luke thought he saw her eyes sparkle, just slightly.

Luke took a deep breath and stood up.

Mr. Kerr, on the other hand, was a jelly doughnut. Or at least what Luke imagined a jelly doughnut would look like if it ever became vice principal of a high school. Rolls of fat bulged in places where most people didn't even have places. He always wore a three-piece suit in some kind of vain attempt to conceal the bulges, but it just made them more obvious. A thick shock of red hair added the jelly to the top of the doughnut.

Kerr's office was dominated by a huge, ugly wooden

desk in the center of the room. The corners of the desk were carved knobs that looked like clenched fists, and the panel in the front was vaguely skull-like in design. The desk was in the middle of a bright circle of light created by four small ceiling-mounted spotlights. Two of the lights shone in Luke's eyes, as if he were a spy under interrogation. *Ve haf vays of making you talk!* he thought.

Kerr was examining a book—*the book*, Luke saw and cringed a little. It had been their English assignment, but after seven attempts, he had given up trying to read it. The remains of the duct tape were still attached to the bottom and spine of the book, covering part of the title so that it said *The Last of the Mo*. Kerr leaned forward and slammed the book down right in front of them, one corner jutting out over the edge of the desk, pointing right at Luke. He and Tommy both stared at it.

Kerr glowered at them from under thick orange eyebrows. "Sit," he said.

They sat.

Luke reached out and straightened the book so that it lined up with the edge of the desk. Kerr looked him in the eye, and Luke quickly glanced away.

"Was it worth it?" Kerr asked.

"Sir?" Tommy asked with an expression of utter innocence.

"Was it worth it?" Kerr repeated.

Luke began, "I'm not sure what—"

"Tell me why I shouldn't call your parents right now. Tell me why I shouldn't call the police."

Luke drew in his breath sharply and caught Ms. Sheck's eyes.

"I don't think there's any need for the police," she said.

Mr. Kerr shot a glance at Ms. Sheck as if she had no right to interfere, but the edges of her mouth curled up into a smile, and even he couldn't bring himself to stay angry with her.

His eyes fastened themselves firmly back on Luke. "I don't know what they let you get away with in New Zealand," Kerr continued, "but in America we have certain standards of behavior that are expected of our students."

Luke considered telling him that he had once been suspended from a school in New Zealand for a "certain standard of behavior" but decided that it wasn't quite the appropriate moment.

Kerr continued. "You have caused this school a lot of embarrassment. You could have been killed."

It wasn't clear which of those two he considered worse.

Kerr started to go on, in the way that vice principals do. Some words filtered through, such as *reckless, impulsive,* and *bad influence,* but the rest of it seemed just to wash over Luke as if Kerr were speaking a foreign language. He kept nodding his head, though, and looking sorry.

It had been a simple enough prank, involving the statue of the school founder, a toilet seat, a roll of toilet paper, a roll of duct tape, and a copy of *The Last of the Mohicans* by James Fenimore Cooper.

Isherwood High was a well-regarded private school founded by a Civil War hero named Jacob Isherwood. A fancy, life-size statue of Isherwood astride his horse sat on a high pedestal out in front of the school. Isherwood was striking an action pose, with one hand on the reins, his rear end raised off the seat, his other hand trailing out behind him as the horse galloped into the distance.

It was Tommy who one day said, "It looks like he's just wiped his ass." But it was Luke who thought of the prank (during a particularly boring history lesson) and convinced Tommy to do it.

They had set out late the previous night and met up at school. By the time they had finished, a copy of *The Last of the Mohicans* was perched in Isherwood's forward hand, as if he were reading it. His rear hand, close to his butt, held a roll of toilet paper, and a toilet seat had been attached to the saddle. The proud statue of the school's founder had been turned into a toilet, and the hero of the Civil War was now reading a book on the can as he galloped into infinity.

They were laughing and climbing down from the statue pedestal when the security patrol drove onto the school grounds. They froze, hoping not to be noticed.

That was when the squirrel, drunk on acorn juice—or maybe it was just the stupidest squirrel in the world—had tripped over its own feet in a nearby tree. It landed on Luke's back, and he leaped off the pedestal with a yell, catching the end of the toilet paper roll in his mouth on the way down.

It unrolled as he fell, twisting out behind him like a parade-day streamer.

Luke hit the ground and froze, with a mouthful of toilet paper and a terrified squirrel clinging to his back. At that point, as his dad would say, the *shoop shoop* really hit the fan.

The next morning, a hundred cell phone cameras snapped the statue, toilet paper and all. By lunchtime it was all over Facebook.

But they would have got away with it, if not for that drunken squirrel.

A fleck of foamy spittle appeared at the corner of Kerr's mouth, and Luke watched it bubble and bounce around with each word.

"We had no choice, sir," Tommy said with an air of wounded dignity when Kerr stopped for breath.

"No choice?" Kerr raised an eyebrow. It looked like a furry orange centipede had just crawled up his forehead.

"No choice," Luke affirmed.

"It's our religion, sir," Tommy said.

Another centipede joined the first. "Your religion."

"Yes, sir." Tommy nodded. "We belong to the Seekers of the Wandering Goat."

Luke nodded with him. "The Wandering Goat."

"You, be quiet." Kerr eyeballed Luke for a second, then turned to Tommy. "Do you boys seriously think you can get away with a prank like this by claiming to be followers of some phony religion?"

"Freedom of religion, sir," Tommy said. "Under the First Amendment, we cannot be persecuted for our religious practices."

"The Seekers of the Wandering Goat . . ." Kerr picked up a file from his desk and leafed through it. "The last time you used this excuse, you were the 'Keepers' of the Wandering Goat. Explain that." He glared at Tommy as if to say, *Gotcha!*

Tommy froze and started going a slightly off shade of white.

Luke jumped in. "The goat escaped."

"It escaped."

"The goat," Tommy agreed.

"Yes, now we're the Seekers of the Wandering Goat," Luke said.

"I guess we weren't very good keepers," Tommy said.

"So where is this goat now?" Kerr asked with a sideways glance at Ms. Sheck, who was clearly trying not to laugh. She pulled her face back into line with an effort.

"If we knew that, sir, we'd be the Keepers of the Wandering Goat again," Tommy said.

"Or maybe the Finders of the Wandering Goat. We haven't decided yet," Luke added.

Kerr picked up the book again. "It seems to me that you went to a lot of trouble just to avoid doing your book project."

"Reading sucks," Luke said without thinking.

"Luke!" Ms. Sheck said.

"I don't think we should be forced to read a book that we don't like, sir," Tommy said. "And this is the most boring book in the world."

"Hey, that's just not true." Ms. Sheck took a step forward, raising her hands as if defending herself. "It's an American classic!"

"They could use it to cure insomnia," Luke said.

"And in hospitals instead of anesthetic," Tommy said.

"It starts a little slow, but it turns into one of the greatest adventures of all time," Ms. Sheck protested.

Kerr picked at a fragment of duct tape on the spine of

the book. "I don't care whether you think it's boring or not. There is just over a week till summer vacation. So this is now your summer project. You have to read it and write a report on it, due to me the first day of school next fall."

"It's a human rights issue," Tommy said.

"Human rights?" Kerr almost sighed.

"It's our right not to die of boredom," Tommy said.

"It really is the most boring book in the world," Luke said, still staring at the book in question, duct tape and all.

"Yes, sir," Tommy said.

"Okay. Let's say I accept that," Kerr said.

Luke risked a quick glance at Tommy, whose mouth had dropped open. This was too easy. Even Ms. Sheck was looking at Kerr with narrowed, confused eyes.

Kerr sprang the trap. "Now all you have to do is prove that it *is* the most boring book in the world."

There was a long pause. Tommy and Luke looked at each other. Kerr smiled triumphantly from behind the desk.

"How exactly would we do that, sir?" Luke asked.

"That's up to you. You prove it, and I'll let you choose another book to read for your project. And I'll accept your crazy Keepers of the—"

"Seekers," Tommy interrupted.

"Seekers of the Wandering Goat story. I'll give you till Tuesday. But if you can't, then I will see to it that you spend your summer break reading the book, and I'm going to come down on you like a ton of bricks for the statue thing."

"Sir, I think we need to define the terms of the agreement," Tommy said.

"I bet if you went on Google and looked up 'the most boring book in the world,' you would find hundreds of books," Ms. Sheck said. "And this one wouldn't even make the list."

"There you go," Kerr said. "If you can find it on an official list of the most boring books in the world, I'll accept that."

"Anywhere on the list?" Luke asked.

"Top ten," Kerr said.

"Sweet as," Luke said.

"Thank you, sir," Tommy said.

"I don't know why you're thanking me. If I were—"

There was a sudden, urgent rap on the door and then it flung open. The school secretary, Mrs. Seddon, stuck her head through the door.

"Yes, Jennifer?" Kerr asked, rather brusquely.

"I'm sorry to bother you, sir," she said. "It's the police on the phone."

"Yes?" Mr. Kerr said, those two orange centipedes scurrying back up his forehead.

Luke felt his back break out in a cold sweat. Had the police somehow been involved already?

But he needn't have worried.

"It's the river," Mrs. Seddon said.

2. THE RAIN

In the months leading up to June in northeastern Iowa, it rained.

And rained.

And rained.

Thunderstorms crashed, colliding with the earth in massive explosions of light and sound and water. Lots of water.

Combined with the thaw from a heavy winter snowfall, it was too much for the saturated soil to cope with. The water began to flow to the rivers.

River levels rose, and rose some more. The Upper Iowa River, the Turkey and Maquoketa Rivers, and catchments of the Wapsipinicon and Iowa Rivers, including the Cedar, Skunk, and Des Moines Rivers.

The residents of those parts, remembering the great floods of '08 and being the sort of folk who took matters into their own hands, got to preparing.

As Luke's dad would tell them many times in the months

afterward, *When the shoop shoop starts flowin', folks get shovelin'.*

And in June in Iowa City, the shoop shoop really started flowing.

So folks got shovelin'.

3. SANDBAGS

The sun was still high in the sky when Luke and Tommy biked over to the river straight after school.

Luke's bike was a loaner from the Iowa City Bike Library. It was old and sturdy but nothing like Tommy's high-tech, carbon-fiber, state-of-the-art, dream-machine bicycle with its computerized gear-changing system and built-in GPS. However, as cool as the bike was, Tommy wasn't happy with it.

At fifteen, they both felt they were too old to be getting around on a bicycle. At least Tommy's parents were going to buy him a motorcycle when he turned sixteen, and Tommy couldn't wait. Luke was sure that whatever motorcycle he got, it would have built-in machine guns, ejector seats, and probably a button that transformed it into a gyrocopter once Tommy was done with it.

Luke had ridden plenty of motorcycles on the farm back home but thought it would be a few years before he (or his parents) could afford one in America.

A trio of ducks was paddling aimlessly over by the far bank, and a light puff of breeze sucked some of the heat out of the afternoon. *Not a bad day,* Luke thought. A day for boating, having a picnic, or playing footy in the riverside park.

Except the riverbank looked like a construction site.

To the left and right, as far as Luke could see, there were people. Hundreds of people, all bustling around with shovels and sacks full of sand. Small front-end loaders were shifting pallets of sandbags toward the beginnings of a wall along the riverbank that would hopefully hold back the floodwaters.

A horn honked behind them as they approached, so they hopped off their bikes and moved to one side to let a truck pass. A fine drift of brown powdery grit was falling from beneath the rear tailgate. The truck stopped and dumped a load of sand in the middle of the street, near a pile of sacks that were bound together with wire.

An old guy with a Nike shirt, Converse sneakers, and a baseball cap on backward was directing the truck with hand signals. *All it would take are a few gold chains and he could be the world's oldest rapper,* Luke thought.

The man noticed them arrive and walked over. Luke had seen him around the campus and the city center before and thought he was probably a professor of some kind. He seemed to be in charge, at least at this bend in the river.

"Volunteers?" the old guy asked.

Tommy nodded a little reluctantly. Physical labor wasn't his strong point.

Luke said, "What can we do?"

"Fill sandbags," the man said. "We could use some help."

"No worries," Luke said. "Where do we start?"

The man pointed at a pile of red-handled shovels lying near the sand heap. "There are work gloves in the cardboard box."

Luke looked at Tommy. "Let's give it a good kick in the guts and see if it moos," he said.

"Kick what? Where?" Tommy shook his head.

Luke grinned.

Tommy locked his bike and Luke's to a post using a high-tech chain that opened with his thumbprint, and they each grabbed a pair of gloves from the box.

"Don't forget to text your folks and tell them where you are," Tommy said.

"Yeah, in a sec," Luke said.

A long wooden tray system stretched from the pile of sand over toward one of the University of Iowa buildings. Spaced out along it at regular intervals were big funnels made out of orange witches' hat–type traffic cones, upside down, with the tops cut off.

The volunteers were working in pairs—one shoveling sand into the base of an upside-down cone, and the other holding a sandbag underneath. When the sandbag was full, they cinched it closed with a plastic tie. Then the two of them carried it over to a pallet. Every now and then, a front-end loader would arrive and pick up a pallet, then carry it down to the river, where a long line of sandbags lay side by side, starting the wall.

"Here, take this," Tommy said, handing Luke what looked

like an MP3 player but, knowing Tommy, probably wasn't. Tommy was wearing a matching one, slung around his neck on a lanyard.

Tommy Wundheiler was going to be a spy someday. He said he was going to work for the CIA, or the NSA, or the DIA, or possibly even the MIC. Luke hadn't even heard of half of those organizations.

Two years ago, when Tommy was thirteen, he had even applied to the CIA to see if they had any positions for spy kids, but they had written back and said they had no openings at the moment. Luke suspected they were just being polite.

Tommy was always buying spy gadgets online.

Luke thought some of the stuff was quite funny, like the Green Gas. You put one drop in someone's food and it made them fart uncontrollably. Or the Sky Spy, which was a kite with a built-in video camera that you flew over your enemies to see what they were up to. Then there was the Brief Safe, designed to hide money or important documents. It looked just like a pair of men's undies and came complete with skid marks so nobody would want to touch it.

It took Tommy a couple of months to save up his allowance for each spy gadget, so there were a lot of things he wanted but hadn't bought yet. It had taken him a whole year to save up for a pair of night-vision goggles that let you see in the dark.

Luke had suggested that when he got his job with the CIA (or the NSA, DIA, MIC, etc.), they would give him the gadgets and he wouldn't have to pay for them. But

Tommy said he didn't want to wait that long.

Now Luke examined the MP3 player closely, trying to work out what secret it was keeping. He couldn't see anything unusual.

"What is it?" Luke asked. "Looks like an MP3 player."

"Looks like, but it isn't," Tommy said mysteriously.

Luke tried to act surprised.

Tommy said, "It's a two-way radio, disguised as an MP3 player. The microphone is hidden here"—it was cleverly concealed about halfway down the earphone cable, where the cable split into two—"and you listen through the earphones. You can have a conversation with someone and people think you are just listening to music."

"Wouldn't they wonder why you were talking to your MP3 player?"

"Just pretend like you're singing along," Tommy said.

"Nobody would believe that," Luke said.

"Why not?"

"Have you ever heard me sing?"

Tommy laughed. Luke slung the gadget around his neck and put on his gloves.

Tommy always had the coolest toys.

"I'll shovel, if you like," Luke said. That looked like the harder of the two jobs.

"I can handle it," Tommy said.

Luke shrugged, then grabbed a sack and held it underneath the cone.

Tommy dug the shovel into the sand and emptied it into the cone.

Luke quickly learned to keep the mouth of the sack tight around the cone; otherwise the sand came out in clouds and got into his mouth and nose and hair.

When the bag was full, they each grabbed an end and hauled it over to the pallet.

"That's one," Luke said.

"That's awesome, dude," Tommy said, and they stood and looked at it for a moment.

"How many do you think we need?" Tommy asked, glancing down at the line of bags by the river.

"That depends on how high they want to build the wall," Luke said. "And how deep. If the base is four sandbags wide and they—"

Tommy held up a hand, stopping him. "One down," he said.

"No worries, bro," Luke said. "Let's finish off the rest and go home."

Down by the river, another group was working in pairs, unloading the sandbags from the pallets and stacking them on the beginnings of the river wall, under the direction of some guys with clipboards and pens, who Luke assumed were engineers from the county.

Even Ms. Sheck turned up after a while, in a tank top and pair of cutoff jeans. She must have gone home to get changed. Her hair had finally escaped from the constraints of school policy and was jutting out at odd angles in all directions. Her wrists were covered with multicolored bangles, and she had a silver stud in the side of her nose and a tattoo of a roaring lion on her upper arm. She would have looked more in place at a rock concert than in a classroom. Luke caught himself staring and quickly turned back to his work.

"Luke, one, two, this is Tommy, three, four. How copy? Over." Tommy's voice sounded in the earpieces of the secret MP3 walkie-talkie.

"I'm standing right here," Luke said.

Tommy stopped digging. He pointed at the walkie-talkie and cupped his ear as if he couldn't hear.

Luke sighed and pressed the hidden TALK button. "Loud and clear, bro."

"Copy that, Luke, one, two," Tommy said, and nodded at Ms. Sheck. "Can you believe she's got a tat? Over."

"She sure looks different without her teacher clothes on," Luke said, waving at her. She smiled, her hands full of sandbag, sharing the load with a guy with his shirt off.

"Oh, and you've seen her without her clothes on?" Tommy said. "Awesome!"

"You wish," Luke said.

"This is her first year teaching," Tommy said. "I wonder what she did before."

"Probably a hired assassin," Luke said.

"Or a spy for the CIA," Tommy said.

"Or a stripper," Luke suggested.

Tommy grinned and dug the shovel back into the sand.

The afternoon wore on. The trucks full of sand kept coming. The piles of sacks did not seem to diminish.

Luke held the sack tightly around the cone and looked across at Tommy. His long flop of black hair was plastered against the side of his head. His T-shirt was soaked in an oval patch across his chest. He was shaking the sand off the shovel into the cone. He seemed to be struggling a bit, and the shovelfuls were starting to come slower.

"My turn," Luke said.

"Nah, I'm good," Tommy said, although clearly he wasn't.

"You're just showing off your muscles for Ms. Sheck," Luke said.

Tommy laughed. "I'd better let you have a turn, then. Give you a chance to impress her."

He handed Luke the shovel and swapped onto the sandpile side of the wooden tray.

It was a simple enough motion: dig the shovel into the sand, twist around to the tray, turn the shovel to empty the sand into the upside-down cone, and turn back to the sandpile.

It took Luke a couple of minutes to settle into a routine, but once he got his rhythm, he found it easy going and, little by little, kept increasing his speed. It was much easier than digging drainage ditches on the farm back home.

Shovel, twist, turn. Shovel, twist, turn.

After a while, a new volunteer, a younger kid Luke didn't know, came to help Tommy move the bags, which left Luke free just to shovel.

They ran out of sandbags after about an hour, and Luke paused for breath. Someone from the city was handing out water bottles, and he took one gratefully. He wiped the sweat off his forehead and noticed a few people staring at him.

He glanced quickly at Tommy, wondering if he had done something wrong, but it turned out to be the opposite.

"You're pretty strong for a little guy," the kid next to him said, shaking his head as if he couldn't quite believe it. There were murmurs of agreement from the crowd.

Luke shrugged it off. He'd dug a lot of ditches on the farm. This was nothing.

"You guys have done almost as many bags as the rest of us put together," the water guy said.

Luke said nothing, embarrassed.

"Show-off," Tommy said, and Luke flicked half a shovelful of sand at him. Tommy laughed and shook it out of his hair. He dug a handful of sand out of his sack and threw it at Luke. For a moment there was a flurry of sand flying back and forth, creating a mini sandstorm over the tray. Then Tommy, his eyes screwed shut against the sand, stumbled and lurched forward.

He put out a foot to regain his balance and crashed into the edge of the wooden tray. It twisted and tipped, then collapsed on itself with a loud crack, spilling sand and witches' hats across the ground.

"Oops," said Tommy.

The old rapper came trotting over. "Who did this?" he demanded.

Tommy raised a hand. "My bad."

"No, it was my fault," Luke said.

Tommy picked up an end of the tray, which was now just a loose heap of timber, and said, "We'll have to fill the sandbags without the cones, I guess."

"That'll be too slow," the old rapper said.

"Give me a sec," Luke said. He grabbed some discarded

wire that had bound the bundles of sacks together. The old man shook his head and wandered off.

"Can you lift up the end?" he asked Tommy. "Hold it together?"

Tommy lifted one end, and Luke grabbed one side and wound a length of wire around it, then crossed over to the other side and twisted the wire tightly around that. He repeated it with another length of wire; then one of the other volunteers found him a heavy screwdriver, which he put between the two wires and twisted around and around. The wires became taut, bit into the wood, and gradually pulled the two sides back into shape around the upside-down cones.

He lashed each side with another length of wire, and did the same for the cracked section in the middle.

He tested it with a good shake. It was more wobbly than before, but it was usable.

The old rapper came back when Luke had finished, and glanced at his work. He said nothing and left.

"That's awesome, dude," Tommy said.

"Us Kiwis can fix the world with a bit of two-by-four and some number eight wire." Luke laughed.

"True dat." Tommy laughed with him, then got back to work.

Later, Luke heard Ms. Sheck singing down by the river. She had a surprisingly good voice. Other people joined in all along the riverbank.

He laughed out loud for no real reason. The ducks were still paddling in circles on the river, the sun was peering through the trees on the far bank, and he was having a really good time. From over by the library building came the smell of cooking. Luke could see smoke where people were setting up barbecues to feed the volunteers.

The river wall was now three or four sandbags high, and the idea that the river could ever rise enough to breach it seemed simply absurd.

4. BENFER

Luke got home after eight. His mother and father were playing Rummikub in the living room, and his dinner was in the microwave.

He was tired but exhilarated. He had helped save the town. A dusting of fine sand drifted from his clothes as he took off his shoes in the entranceway. He saw his mother notice, so he quickly got the brush and dustpan from the hall cupboard and swept up the mess.

For someone who had lived on a farm most of her life, she was extraordinarily tidy. The floors were vacuumed twice a day, the windows were washed weekly, and heaven help any male in the household who forgot to put the toilet seat (and lid) down after using it.

Never flush with the lid open, she'd say. *You might as well spray crap all around the room.* (His mother's fussiness when it came to housework did not extend to language.)

"Hi, Mum. Hi, Dad."

"You're filthy!" his mother said. "Where have you been?"

"Down at the river, helping out with the sandbagging," Luke said.

"Couldn't you have texted us," his father said, "to let us know where you were?"

Luke winced. "Oh, yeah, I was gonna. I just forgot."

"You forgot." His mother shook her head.

"You can remember the score of every All Blacks rugby game ever played," his father said, "but you can't remember to text us when you're going to be home late."

"Sorry," Luke said.

It was true. He could remember almost everything—phone numbers, sports scores, the license plates of every car they'd ever had. If you gave him a handful of dollar bills and let him flick through them, he could write down each of the serial numbers and get it right. And yet half the time he couldn't remember what day of the week it was.

"You'd forget your head if it wasn't screwed on," his mother said.

"I'll run upstairs and shower," Luke said.

"Just before you do that . . . ," his father said.

"Yeah?"

"Your school rang this afternoon. The vice principal."

"Mr. Kerr. Oh . . ." Luke looked at his socks.

"Yes, 'oh,'" his father said.

"Sorry about that," Luke muttered.

"It's like your last school all over again," his father said.

"Sorry, Dad."

"Luke, you can't afford to get expelled. The university

pays your fees at this school, and we can't afford to pay your fees elsewhere."

Luke's mother's eyes switched from Luke to his father when the conversation turned to money.

"It really wasn't that big a—"

His father cut him off. "And what if they involve the police? If you get arrested, you could get deported to New Zealand, and that would mean we'd all have to go."

Luke shut his mouth abruptly. It had never occurred to him that a stupid joke could result in their getting booted out of the country. That would be disastrous.

His family had been flat broke for a couple of years, since they were forced to sell the farm back in New Zealand. Even here in Iowa they were living in a dingy, creepy old house while his father tried to pay off his debts. They couldn't even afford a TV.

"Sorry," he said.

"Why do you do these things?" his mother asked.

"I just don't think, I guess," Luke said. "I always feel bad about it later."

"You were born with a perfectly good brain. Why don't you use it?" his father asked.

Luke shrugged.

"I sometimes think you were born with two brains," his mother said. "Like the rabbit and the tortoise."

"The hare," Luke said.

"Whatever it is. You have a hare brain that makes you jump into anything without thinking, and a tortoise brain that allows you to slowly catch up, but always much too late."

"That's not quite the point of the hare and tortoise story, Mum."

"Next time try to engage your other brain. The one that thinks about things before rushing into them," his mother said.

"I'll try."

There was a pause and Luke waited. His father's usual way was to hit him with the bad news, then try to end with something softer. To finish on a positive note.

"It was good work down by the river today, Luke," his father said. "I heard about it through Philipp Khodier over in Physics. He said you were working really hard."

Luke wondered if Philipp was the old rapper with the backward baseball cap.

"Easy as," he said. "Just like digging ditches back on the farm."

"Well, good on you anyway. If it wasn't for that, we'd be grounding you for the other thing. So count your blessings."

"And run upstairs for your shower," his mother reminded him.

"Thanks, Dad. Thanks, Mum," Luke said, and turned to go upstairs.

It was almost an hour later before he got to borrow his dad's computer for his homework.

Kerr's ultimatum had gone from his mind while they had worked at the river. But at home, reality struck, and he knew that he was in deep trouble if he couldn't come up with something.

The most boring book in the world. He typed it into Google and hit ENTER.

There were a bunch of entries, from websites to blogs, all just individuals expressing their opinions on some book or other that they had read and did or didn't like.

He flicked through the first few pages of results, looking for a complete list, the way some movie sites had lists of the best and worst movies of all time. But page after page, nothing looked like it would be useful.

The entry that finally caught his attention took him to an online encyclopedia article, and intrigued despite himself, he began to read.

The Most Boring Book in the World

Leonardo's River, a novel by nineteenth-century New England inventor Darcy Benfer, is considered by many historians to be the most boring book ever printed. Its claim to this status is unproven, however, and disputed by other scholars.

Publication

Leonardo's River was written and published by Darcy Benfer in the town of Longmeadow, Massachusetts, in 1853. Only one copy of the book was ever printed, due to a fire at the printer that destroyed the original manuscript and all of the printed pages of the book except for the copy that had been sent to the author for checking.

Accounts suggest that the printing press operator began to read the book while printing it and fell asleep, leading to the fire that destroyed the printery.[citation needed]

Cover

The cover of *Leonardo's River* contains just the title of the book above a reproduction of Leonardo da Vinci's drawing *Vitruvian Man.*

Reception

Few, if any, people are recorded as having read the book, partly due to the fact that there was only one copy available, and partly due to the difficulty of reading it.

Luke skipped over the rest of the article, as it didn't really help his case. He was about to close the page when a final note caught his eye.

The only printed copy of the book was donated by Mr. Benfer to the Franklin Public Library in Franklin,

Massachusetts, in 1857. Thirty years later, a search of the library storage areas failed to find a copy of the book, and it has been missing ever since.

In 1995, millionaire book collector James Mullins offered five hundred thousand dollars for a copy of *Leonardo's River.* This was later increased to two million dollars. The reward was never claimed. The book's value is due to its rarity and also to its notoriety as the most boring book ever published.

Two million dollars! Luke shook his head, his eyes wide. Two million dollars for a book that was so boring nobody could read it.

But it still didn't help his case. He tried a couple of different search engines, but none of them listed *The Last of the Mohicans* as among the most boring books in the world. Most of them said good stuff about it.

It looked like he would be spending his summer break reading the book and writing a huge book report on it. Then there would come the punishment for the statue prank.

That all seemed like a disaster, but as it turned out, the reality was much worse.

5. DARK WATERS RISING

After school the next day, Luke talked Tommy into returning to the riverbank.

It had clouded over, and the air was thick and humid. The clouds to the north were black with the threat of heavy rain.

The river had darkened from its normal coffee color to dark chocolate. It was higher, too, already lapping at the tops of the river embankments and threatening to spill over toward the near-finished sandbag levee. It was running faster, as if it were trying to escape from some unseen horror. It smelled strange also, a vaguely putrid stench of pollution and decay.

"Danger close, danger close, contact three o'clock," Tommy said suddenly as they neared the river.

Luke looked over to see Mr. Kerr sitting in his car, a tiny red Daihatsu, surveying the work along the riverbank.

"How does he even get into that thing?" Luke wondered out loud. The car looked smaller than Kerr.

"Must take a can opener to get him out," Tommy said.

They quickened their pace, hoping to get past before Kerr spotted them, but they were too late.

"Good afternoon, boys," Kerr greeted them grimly, winding down the window.

They stopped pedaling and drifted to a halt alongside him.

"Any luck with your research?" he asked. "As per our agreement?"

Tommy shook his head.

"We haven't had much time to do the research yet," Luke said. "We were helping out here at the river yesterday after school."

"You may need to recheck your priorities," Kerr said.

"But the river's going to flood," Tommy said, gesturing toward it. "What could be more important than that?"

"The school board is baying for blood," Kerr said. "They want you suspended. I've told them that I've given you one chance, and I'll stick by that, but if you don't come up with something, you should look at finding new schools next semester."

He started the engine and drove off.

"Plonker," Luke said.

"Jerk," Tommy agreed.

"I don't see *him* staying to help," Luke said.

"He'd be useless anyway," Tommy said.

"I don't know," Luke said. "He'd make a pretty good sandbag."

They both laughed as they made their way down to the riverbank, but the laughter quickly faded.

There was no singing today. The carnival atmosphere of yesterday had vanished somewhere with the blue skies and sunshine. A lot of the volunteers seemed to be just standing around, waiting for truckloads of sand to arrive.

"Will it get much worse than this?" Luke heard someone ask.

"A little, maybe," another voice said. "But the sandbags will hold any spillage. As long as the Coralville Dam holds."

Luke rubbed his palms together while they waited for something to do. His skin was red and a little raw. It had been a while since he had done so much physical work, and his hands weren't used to it.

Tommy had Band-Aids on his palms, and Luke wouldn't have blamed him if he had not wanted to help today, but he had still shown up. That was Tommy.

The old rapper appeared next to them. He pointed to the library building. "Could use you in the library today," he said. "They're trying to rescue as many books as they can from the basement."

"Great!" Tommy said.

"Hmm," Luke said.

Libraries made Luke nervous. They were full of books, and that seemed like far too much reading all concentrated in one place to him. As if it would reach critical mass and start a chain reaction and explode in a huge blast of words and sentence fragments.

The university library was a large brick building, barely a hundred yards from the river. Between the library and the rapidly rising waters were just a parking lot and a railway line.

Luke and Tommy walked in through the main entrance.

Claudia Smith was in charge. Luke knew her from one of his mother's community groups. She had been around to their place for coffee.

She smiled when she saw Luke and said, "Thanks for coming."

"No worries," Luke replied. "How can we help?"

There was a small crowd of volunteers in the main entrance and hallway of the library. For a small crowd, they were making a lot of noise, and Claudia clapped her hands for quiet.

"We don't anticipate any flooding or damage from this level upward," she said in a strong, clear voice. "The problem is in the basement, where we store our specialty and rare book collections, and the university archives." There was silence and she looked around at the volunteers. "There are valuable rare books and historical documents down there. Some of them are the only copies, so we have to move them up to higher levels."

That sounds pretty easy, Luke thought.

She continued. "The problem is that they're in storage areas in the basement, and space is very tight. We can't get book trucks in there."

Luke wasn't sure what a book truck was, but thought it might be one of the wooden trolleys he had seen library staff wheeling around.

Claudia Smith was not smiling now. "So thank you for volunteering," she said. "Some of you can help stack the books, and some can help carry, but the entrance and the corridors are very narrow, so we can get only a few people in there to work."

"How are you going to move all those books with just a few people?" someone asked.

"We're not sure," Claudia said. "In that confined space, without book trucks, well . . . there's simply no way. We have some experts flying in tomorrow who are going to look at removing part of one of the walls so we can extract books that way. And a firm in Washington has a portable robotic conveyor belt system that might help, but they can't get it here and assemble it before Friday, which may be too late. We will try and move as many of the rarest books as we can. The rest . . ." She stopped, clearly upset.

Luke had never seen someone who cared so much about a bunch of old books before.

There was an uncomfortable silence for a moment until Luke had an idea and put his hand in the air.

"Yes, Luke?" she asked.

"What you need is a bucket brigade," he said.

"Bucket brigade?" she asked.

"Yeah, like in the olden days when there was a fire," he said. "A human chain—just pass the books from one person to another."

There was a murmur of agreement around them, but Claudia said doubtfully, "We'd need hundreds of people to make a line all the way up here from down in the base-ment."

"There're heaps of people sitting around by the river," Luke said. "I'll trot back and round a few up."

"Well," she said, "I guess . . . that'd be great. It might even work."

Luke and Tommy were at the head of a long line of volunteers, following Claudia down a narrow flight of concrete stairs into the library's basement. A wide corridor stretched into the distance, lined with boxes and shelves in odd places. Wires and cables ran along the walls. Overhead, what looked like an upside-down conveyor belt was attached to the ceiling and extended the length of the corridor.

Luke looked at it as they walked but couldn't quite figure it out.

"What do you reckon that is?" he asked Tommy.

"It's a conveyor belt," Tommy said.

"Yeah, but it's upside down. If you put anything on that, it would fall off."

"If you had a brain cell, it would fall off," Tommy said. "We're just looking at it from underneath, moron."

Claudia must have overheard, because she said, "He's right."

"See, dude?" Tommy said. "You *are* a moron."

"How many fingers am I holding up?" Luke flipped him the bird but grinned at the same time.

Claudia gave them both a disapproving glance and said, "About the conveyor belt. It's used to move returned books from the north entrance back to the processing office."

The corridor twisted and turned, and they arrived at a concrete block wall with lots of green doors. Next to each door frame was a black metal plate with a number engraved into it, and that number was repeated on each door in white lettering.

Claudia produced a key and unlocked a door marked 6043.

Luke waited his turn to enter, then stepped inside and instantly drew in his breath. Beside him, he heard Tommy do the same.

For what looked like hundreds of yards in front of them, a narrow corridor led between two enormous shelving units that were packed with books from floor to ceiling. To his left and right, as far as the eye could see, more units reached out into the distance. There were more books here than Luke could possibly imagine, and if Claudia thought they were going to move all of those upstairs in a couple of days, she was sadly mistaken—even with his bucket brigade idea.

She must have read his thoughts. She said, "We'll concentrate on the lower shelves and on the rare or older sections. Librarians will select the books and pass them, one at a time, to the first person in the line. They'll pass them to the person next to them, and so on, all the way up to the third level, where other library staff will decide how to stack them."

The crowd began to sort itself out into a single long line. A human conveyor belt.

Luke found himself alongside a dark metal cage. A thin-faced university student stood to his right, Tommy was to his left, and, to his surprise, Ms. Sheck took the place to the left of Tommy.

"Hi, Ms. S," Luke said.

"Hi, Luke. Hi, Tommy," she said.

"Nice tat," Tommy said with a grin.

She went a little red and instinctively moved her hand to cover the lion on her arm.

"No, really," Luke said, "it looks cool."

"Yeah, Luke's getting one just like it," Tommy said.

"You are not!" she said, laughing.

"Yeah, he is, with your name underneath," Tommy said.

It was Luke's turn to feel his cheeks go red. "Piss off," he said.

Ms. Sheck laughed.

They waited for a while. Nothing happened at first. Luke guessed the librarians were organizing themselves inside the storage room.

"How did you boys do with *The Last of the Mohicans*?" Ms. Sheck asked. "Did you find it on Google?"

It was pretty clear that she doubted they would. Luke debated for a moment whether to tell her about the most boring book in the world but decided not to.

"Not yet," Tommy said. "But I'm sure it will be there."

"We've been busy," Luke said. "We've been down at the river, helping out."

Ms. Sheck nodded. "I know. I'll put in a good word for you with Mr. Kerr."

"It won't help," Luke said. Just then, the first book arrived and he turned to take it.

The first book looked like an encyclopedia and must have been, because it was immediately followed by another identical book and another. Thirty-six of them in all, each numbered, although he couldn't read the titles, as they were in some foreign language. There were lots of consonants, so it might have been Dutch, or German, or Swiss. He asked Tommy.

Tommy's family was from the Amana community of Iowa, a historic German religious group. And although his grandparents had left the community back in the 1930s, his family had kept its native language. Tommy was as fluent in German as he was in English.

"Not German," he said. "I think it's Dutch."

Luke took each book that was passed to him and handed it on to Tommy. It wasn't hard work although the books started to come faster and faster as the workers settled into a routine.

Book after book flew through his hands. From Luke to Tommy to Ms. Sheck. Big books, small books, old books, modern-looking books. Archival cartons that were full of papers and quite heavy. The stream of books seemed endless, and still he felt they were merely scratching the surface of the mountain behind the painted green door.

He hadn't really imagined that there were so many books in the world, and it occurred to him that the amount of knowledge that had passed through his hands in just a few hours must have been phenomenal.

His father had once written a book, a practical guide to dairy farming, so Luke knew how much work went into it. Each book he handed Tommy had been researched, written, edited, proofread, and finally published, no doubt celebrated with a party and a launch for the book, only for it to end up, years later, locked in a concrete dungeon in the basement of the university library.

It seemed sad, in a way.

The hours went quickly. The hand-over-hand action of conveying the books kept them busy, and simple chat filled in the time.

"What did you do before you were a teacher?" Luke asked Ms. Sheck with a sideways glance at Tommy.

She shrugged. "I had a couple of jobs."

"What did you do?" Luke asked.

"Oh, you know . . ." She shook her head. "Just something different."

"Were you, like, an assassin?" Luke asked.

She laughed. "No, nothing like that."

"Or a stri—" The words were choked off in Tommy's throat as Luke's elbow caught him in the ribs.

"But it must have been something really secret if you can't tell us about it," Luke rushed out before Ms. Sheck could catch what Tommy had been about to say.

"Or really embarrassing," Tommy said, still a little winded.

She shook her head. "No, nothing secret or embarrassing."

"Then why are you avoiding telling us?" Luke asked.

"I'm not."

"You are."

"Okay, then."

"Well?" Luke asked.

"I was a singer," she said.

"A singer? Awesome! What kind of music?" Tommy asked.

"I sang lead vocals for a local jazz band, and I had a

six-week gig in Vegas one year as a backup singer for Michael Bolton."

"I thought you said it was nothing embarrassing," Luke said.

"Why'd you give it up?" Tommy asked.

There was a long pause; then Ms. Sheck said, "I cut a single. Just me. A song I wrote, arranged, and performed. It got some local airplay and that was that. I sold thirty-seven copies at the local record store, and it was illegally downloaded about a hundred and fifty times. What with all the late nights, it seemed like too much hard work to me, so I gave it up and got my teacher certification."

"Wow!" Luke said. "You got a copy of it? I'd love to hear—"

A dusty gray book with a tattered cover passed through his hands so quickly that he almost didn't notice it.

Almost.

But he did.

When he took it, it was upside down, but for reasons that he could never quite understand afterward, he turned it over as he gave it to Tommy. Tommy's hands covered the title, but Luke had just enough time to register the spidery line drawing of a man in a circle, his arms and legs outstretched, and then the book was gone, on to Ms. Sheck and the next person, disappearing around the corner and out of sight.

Luke stopped taking books and jumped out of line, causing a momentary disruption in the flow.

"What are you doing?" Tommy asked, frowning.

"Nothing," he said, red-faced, getting back in the line.

He hadn't been able to see the title of the book, but he had certainly seen the picture.

The man in the circle! The *Vitruvian Man.* That was supposedly the picture on the front cover of *Leonardo's River*—the two-million-dollar book!

Tommy's hands had obscured the title, but he had seen the first letter. The letter *L.*

"Get a grip, dude," Tommy said, and Luke realized that he had slowed down and was still holding up the line. He forced himself to concentrate on what he was doing, but his mind would not let it go.

Could it have been *Leonardo's River*?

If it was, why didn't the library know they had it? According to the website he'd read, the only known copy of the book was missing.

As he was pondering this, there was a commotion from around the corner toward the storeroom. Luke heard someone say, "Don't panic," and thought that when people say that, there is always a reason *to* panic.

Claudia appeared, looking stressed, a cell phone in her hand.

"There's no need to panic," she said, not reassuring Luke at all. "But we've just lost the dam at Coralville."

"Has it burst?" Tommy asked, wide-eyed.

"No, no, nothing like that," Claudia said. "It's overflowed. They've lost control of the river level, and it looks like a flood is certain. We need to evacuate. Stay calm," she said.

But she didn't sound very calm.

6. THE VITAMIN MAN

"You gotta be kidding," Tommy said for the third time. "Two million bucks!"

"If it is the book," Luke said.

"The dumbest book in the world," Tommy said.

"The most *boring* book in the world," Luke corrected him. "And I didn't see the title of the book, just the illustration on the front cover."

"So you don't even know if it is that book?"

Luke sighed. "On the cover of the boring book is a drawing of this nude dude in a circle. It's a famous picture by that da Vinci bloke."

"I know it," Tommy said. "It's called the *Vitamin Man* or something like that."

"The *Vitruvian Man*," Luke said.

"There could be thousands of books with that picture on the cover," Tommy said.

"Give me a piece of paper and a pencil," Luke said. He

closed his eyes for a moment, replaying the movie inside his head of the book chain in the basement. He saw the glare of the fluorescent lights and felt the pressure of the deep concrete walls. He smelled the dust of old paper and watched as book after book traveled past. Then came the gray cloth-covered book. He watched it turn over as he handed it to Tommy, and pressed PAUSE on his mental movie player.

"Here you go, dude." Tommy was back with a pencil and some paper.

Luke sketched the picture that was inside his head. He drew Tommy's fingers splayed across the cover and the glimpses of other letters that peeked through between them.

"It could be," Tommy said, examining it. "You sure this picture is right?"

"I'm sure," Luke said, tapping the side of his head.

"How do you do that?" Tommy asked.

"Dunno, bro," Luke said.

After the excitement at the library, they had gone around to Tommy's house, which was big and luxurious and over-looked the river, although it was on high ground and safe from any flood. It couldn't be more different from Luke's house, which was located on the other side of the river and was three stories high, ancient, and creepy, like the house out of *Psycho*.

Tommy's whole house was filled with cool toys. He had the latest PlayStation and an Xbox, both of which were connected to a television that seemed to take up an entire wall. Each room was connected by a video intercom. All the windows opened or closed at the push of a button and automatically shut if it rained (like now).

It wasn't the first time that Luke had been to Tommy's house, but each time he went, he shook his head in amazement.

Luke was staying at Tommy's that night. Tommy's parents were out and not due back till late, something to do with the flood, so Luke and Tommy had microwaved some frozen pizza for dinner.

It was raining heavily, and through the big plate-glass windows of the living room, they could barely make out the streetlights that lined the riverbanks. As night had fallen, the shapeless black mass between the banks had seemed to come alive, and malevolent. The river had already climbed over its banks, but it was still held in check by the sandbag barrier that they had all helped to create.

The streetlights illuminated the barrier, and they could see the swell of the river, rising slowly, creeping up the sandbags one by one.

"All we have to do is check the library website," Tommy said at last. "Every book in the library is catalogued electronically."

"You sure?" Luke asked.

Tommy nodded.

"Even the rare and specialty ones?" Luke asked.

"You bet. They're the hardest ones to keep track of, because of how they're stored in the basement."

"But the electricity is out in the library," Luke said. "They shut it down after we evacuated."

"What's your point?"

"How can we access their website when all their computers are shut down?"

Tommy rolled his eyes. "Their website is not on a computer in the library, moron. It'll be on a big server in a data center somewhere, maybe not even in Iowa."

"I knew that," Luke said. He actually had known that, if he had bothered to think before opening his mouth.

"So let's find out," Tommy said.

Tommy had his own laptop, with a wireless connection. He got it from his bedroom and put it down on the carpet in front of them.

"What was the name again?" he asked, typing in the address of the university library site.

"*Leonardo's River,*" Luke said, and spelled it out to make sure Tommy got it right.

"Nothing," Tommy said a minute later. "I'll try some variations on the spelling in case it's been catalogued wrong." After a while, he said, "Nope, nothing, zip."

"Try the author," Luke suggested, and Tommy did, but that also proved fruitless.

"Must have been some other book," Tommy said. "One with a similar cover."

"Nope," Luke said. "I'm sure it was the book."

"It's probably just because you'd read about the book yesterday; then you saw a book that looked a bit similar, so your mind put two and two together and got six," Tommy surmised.

"But what if it was the book?" Luke said. "That would be

cool. To find a book that has been lost for over a hundred years."

Tommy nodded. "Even if it is the most boring book in the world." He jumped up suddenly. "Hang on, we might be able to find out."

"How?"

"Follow me."

Tommy led the way to a room at the rear of the house, away from the river.

"Mom has all kinds of books about books," he said. "Maybe one of them will have a picture of the cover."

Tommy's mother was a professor in the English department of the university.

Tommy opened a door and flicked on a light switch. Outside, lightning flashed and thunder roared.

"Do that again," Luke said, and Tommy flicked the light switch off and on again.

Almost immediately, lightning lit up the skies, and the house shook with thunder.

"You always have the coolest toys," Luke said, following Tommy into the room.

It was Tommy's parents' private library, stacked floor to ceiling with books, neatly arranged on shelves of varying heights.

"Why would anyone want so many books?" Luke asked, but Tommy ignored him.

"Give me a hand," he said. Tommy ran his finger along the spines, clearly not quite sure what he was looking for.

Luke sighed and started on the other side of the room.

The section he was looking in had a long row of classics, like Shakespeare and Dickens. He had just found a shelf of poetry, with names such as Longfellow and Wordsworth on the spines, when Tommy said, "Here we go."

Lightning flashed again, and rain hammered against the window. Luke was glad they'd made it back before the storm had hit.

Tommy was flipping through a large cloth-covered book titled *A Guide to Rare and Lost Books*.

"Did you know that a first edition of Shakespeare's collected works from 1623 is estimated at six million dollars?" Tommy said.

Luke whistled. Compared to that, *Leonardo's River* was a bargain.

Tommy continued. "An original copy of the Declaration of Independence is worth eight million, but the rarest book in the world is the Gutenberg Bible. It was published in 1456 and was the first book ever printed. A complete first edition today is worth twenty-five to thirty million dollars!"

"Got a copy of that at home," Luke said casually.

"Yeah, right."

"We use it to prop up the coffee table with the wonky leg."

Tommy laughed.

"What about *Leonardo's River*?" Luke asked.

"Hang on," he said, still reading. "Get this. Remember your buddy da Vinci? If you found an original collection of Leonardo da Vinci's manuscripts, they could be worth as much as a hundred million dollars!"

Luke thought about that for a moment, wondering what he'd spend that kind of money on.

Tommy skipped to another section in the book and ran a finger down the page. "He was a famous artist and scientist, born in 1452. He painted the *Mona Lisa*—that's that picture of the lady with the funny smile—"

"I know what the *Mona Lisa* looks like," Luke said.

"And another famous painting called *The Last Supper*. Plus he invented all kinds of things, years ahead of his time."

"Like what?" Luke asked.

Tommy turned the book around and showed Luke some pictures. "Submarines, helicopters, tanks, machine guns, solar power, stuff that didn't exist until hundreds of years later."

"That's unreal," Luke said. "But what about *Leonardo's River?*"

"Here it is," Tommy said. "A whole page on it, and there's a picture of the cover."

He held up Luke's drawing, comparing it to the picture in the book.

Luke wrenched the book from him and stared closely at it. "That's the book I saw in the library," he said.

"Are you sure?" Tommy asked.

"Does a cow lift its tail to fart?"

Tommy raised an eyebrow. "Is that a yes?"

"Yes."

"Wow. What are we going to do?" Tommy asked.

"About what?" Luke looked at him blankly.

"The book, moron."

"What do you mean?"

"Are you kidding me?" Tommy stabbed a finger at the picture of the cover. "That book has been lost for over a hundred years. It's worth two million bucks. We should go get it."

"Why?"

"Dude!" Tommy said. "The library doesn't even know they've got it. It's been lost in their basement for decades. They're not going to miss it."

Luke looked squarely at him. "It's still stealing, bro."

"Finders keepers, if you ask me," Tommy said.

"Yeah, but—"

"Your share would be a million bucks," Tommy said, and that shut Luke up.

Luke thought of their dingy old house that didn't even have a TV.

A million dollars would change their lives.

"We'll have to cross the river," Luke said.

All the bridges had been closed for over an hour.

7. BAD MOON

By the time they got to the footbridge, Luke was soaked, despite the heavy parka that Tommy had lent him. It was too big, and water got into places that water wasn't supposed to get into. It trickled down the side of his neck and the small of his back. He was glad Tommy hadn't insisted on their wearing the secret MP3 radios. They would have been soaked and ruined by now.

But water wasn't a problem. Wet would dry. The thunder and lightning, however, took a little more getting used to.

They say that everything is bigger in America, and the thunderstorms seemed to take pride in that fact. The lightning was hunting in packs, vast sheets of it striking in quick succession in different corners of the sky. At times it was almost constant, the world around them flickering with the strobelike quality of an old black-and-white movie.

Thunder buffeted them from every direction, the waves of sound crashing and building on each other like breakers on a beach. The distant thunder came in long drumrolls, but the closer claps sounded like explosions.

Usually, after dark, the bridge was lit up with dozens of large white globes standing on tall poles. But tonight the lights were all off. It seemed like an ominous sign, although it probably suited their purpose of trying to sneak across the river without being seen. Luke didn't know whether the authorities had turned the lights off or whether the water had shorted some wiring somewhere. Along the riverbank on each side, the lights were still on, shimmering through the pounding rain.

Enough light filtered through the trees that he could see the start of the bridge, where it joined the pathway through the park. Something was moving on each side of it, and he realized with horror that it was water.

The water was normally about fifteen feet below the footbridge, but now it was lapping at its underside.

"Get down," Tommy hissed, and Luke dropped to one knee.

"Contact nine o'clock!" Tommy motioned toward the auditorium to their left. "Gotta be a cop!"

Luke could see a flashlight bobbing and swinging with the gait of the person carrying it, occasionally splaying over the side of the large building.

"We've got to go now," Luke whispered hoarsely, "before he gets to the bridge."

"Maybe we should . . . ," Tommy started, but Luke was already moving.

It was probably just his imagination, but the rain seemed worse on the bridge.

On this side of the river, trees overhung the bridge, and in the dim light he could see tree trunks sprouting out of the water where the riverbank used to be, swaying with the motion of the river. Their leaves and branches reached down, clutching at Luke and Tommy with spiny twig fingers, then pulling back, only to reach for them again, a little closer each time.

They crept across the blackened footbridge, the sounds of the river right at their feet. The putrid smell Luke had noticed earlier in the day was much stronger now. The river reeked like a sewer.

"Who farted, dude?" Tommy said. "That's disgusting."

Luke glanced back to see not one, but two police officers silhouetted by the lights in the park beyond the bridge.

They reached the center of the span, heads bowed against the rain. Here in the middle of the river, the wind was in a fury, hurling blasts of water at them as if trying to sweep them from the bridge.

Lightning flashed again, right on the riverbank, not three hundred feet downstream. It struck a tree, and there was a crack, followed by a strange creaking noise, audible even above the crashing thunder and the rush of the water, as about half the tree split away and toppled into the river.

Immediately, flashlights came on along the opposite bank. More police. Two of them, spotlighting the riverbank, searching for the source of the noise.

"Contact front!" Tommy said, twisting his head toward Luke to be heard.

Luke looked behind him. They were stuck. They couldn't go forward and they couldn't go backward.

"Well, this was one of your better ideas," Tommy said.

"I thought it was your idea," Luke said.

He glanced both ways desperately, hoping the officers would head off somewhere. But clearly they were there to stop anybody stupid enough to try crossing the bridge.

"We'll have to wait for them to leave," Luke shouted, the wind swallowing up the words and spitting them upriver.

Even as he spoke, there was an angry surge, and black water spilled across the concrete base of the bridge, flowing around Luke's shoes in the darkness.

"I hope you can swim," Tommy yelled.

His words were cut off by another brilliant flash of light, searing their eyeballs. Then two giant hands of thunder shook the sturdy bridge and them with it.

At that moment, the moon appeared through a hole, a deep tunnel in the clouds. It wasn't a full moon, and it came and went as dark cloud curtains were drawn again and again across its face, but it still lit them up like actors on a stage.

"Go away!" Luke shouted at the sky, certain that the police would see them. "Bad moon! Go away!"

More water surged across the base of the bridge. The river was rising faster now, and as he watched, the bridge beneath their feet disappeared into the river, leaving just the handrail to either side sticking up out of the water.

Luke grabbed the rail for balance and Tommy did the same. Water gushed up over the tops of Luke's shoes.

"We gotta get moving," Tommy yelled.

"You think?" Luke shouted back.

They'd made it only a couple of yards when that bad

moon burst back into life. There was a shout from the far bank, and two powerful flashlights illuminated them like prison fugitives.

There was shouting, too, and although Luke couldn't make out the words, it was pretty obvious what they wanted.

He gripped the handrail, fighting to keep his feet against the rush of the water, which now reached up just below his knees.

Tommy slipped and fell, and if not for Luke's hand on the neck of his parka, he would have gone under.

Luke hauled him back up and clutched the handrail with both hands, inching his way forward.

Then Luke's footing went. One minute he was standing, and the next minute his knee cracked into the struts of the handrail with a sickening thud, and a jagged spear of pain shot up his leg. He kept hold of the handrail, though, thinking that if it weren't for that, they'd be a mile downstream by now. He hauled himself back to his feet, his shoes jammed up against the bottom of the handrail by the force of the water.

Tommy stopped, grasping the railing, unable to move.

Around them the river was not simply flowing; it was seething and boiling, massive currents pushing their way to the surface.

"I'm stuck," Tommy yelled.

"Hand over hand," Luke shouted. "Just pull yourself along!"

Tommy reluctantly took one hand off the rail and replaced it in front of the other. Luke put a hand on his friend's shoulders to steady him and urged him on.

They moved what seemed like an inch at a time, but still they moved. The surge of the water seemed to lessen as they neared the far bank.

The cops waded into the river and extended their hands to help them the last few feet, dragging them out of the water. They didn't let go until Luke and Tommy were up onto higher, drier ground, away from the river and the bridge approach.

"What the hell do you think you're doing?" one of the police officers shouted into Luke's face.

"Are you completely insane?" asked the other one.

"We . . . we were . . . ," Tommy stammered, gasping for breath.

"We got lost," Luke said.

"Lost!" It was clear the police officer didn't believe him. "I want your names and addresses, and I want to know what you were really doing out there."

"We were looking for my sister," Tommy said, and Luke glanced sharply at him. "She's only six."

"Your sister? Where?"

The alarm on the police officers' faces was instant.

"She was behind us," Tommy said, waving a hand in that general direction.

The police officers turned their lights back to the river, forgetting about Luke and Tommy, their concentration on the dark, rushing waters that consumed the footbridge.

The moment the police officers turned, Tommy and Luke ran, sprinting through the rain up the sloping path that led away from the river. There were shouts and footsteps behind them, but Tommy and Luke were smaller and quicker and had a head start. They ducked off the path into the cover of some trees and crouched, watching as heavy boots thundered up the pathway.

As soon as the cops were past, they cut back down through the trees to the river path and, with water lapping at their feet, ran down the pathway until they reached a covered entrance to one of the university buildings. Out of the rain and away from danger—for the moment, at least. They both collapsed onto a set of concrete stairs that led up to the doorway.

Tommy whooped with excitement. "You think we lost them?"

Luke nodded.

"How's the leg?"

"Just a bang. Bit of a gash. I've had worse."

"You'd better rinse it off real good. That water smelled like seven sorts of sh —"

"Shoop shoop." Luke grimaced. "Tasted like it, too."

"I told you not to drink the stuff," Tommy said.

"What can I say? I was thirsty," Luke said.

"We were lucky twice tonight," Tommy said. He leaned back on the stairs and stretched out his legs. "With the river, then with the cops."

"True that." Luke reached out of the shelter and cupped his hands, collecting some rainwater. He rinsed his mouth and spat it out, trying to clear the acrid taste from his tongue.

"Shame about the book, though. I was really looking forward to finding it," Tommy said.

"Me too."

"I mean, if it was up to me, I'd still be heading in there, but with your sore leg . . ."

"My leg's sweet as, bro," Luke said.

"And all the water you swallowed and everything?"

"No, I'm good."

"I mean, I'd be going for it. But I don't blame you if you want to just head home," Tommy said.

"What for?"

"You know. Warm bath, hot chocolate, and a nap."

"My grandmother likes warm baths, hot chocolates, and naps," Luke said.

"You seriously still want to break into the library?"

"Absolutely. As soon as the floods go down, that book will be locked away in the basement and all the electricity and security cameras and alarms will be turned back on. It's now or never."

"What if we get caught?" Tommy asked.

"It's a library," Luke said. "What are they going to do— tell us to shush? Come on."

They made sure the coast was clear, then headed toward the library. The rain was heavy and constant, but Luke didn't mind because it washed away some of the muck and the stench of the river water.

"Look at it this way," Luke said as they walked. "The hard bit is over now."

He was wrong about a lot of things that night.

8. DOG-FACE

Red lights of fire engines reflected off the wet roads
and strobed the walls of the library. There were other
colors, too, orange lights of emergency vehicles and the
red-blue lights of police cars all intermingling. The rain
caught the lights so that it seemed even the air around
them was dancing in a crazy circus disco of colors and
patterns.

Police officers, firefighters, and security guards stood
around in groups, talking and gesturing at the river, paying
no attention to the rain.

"We'll never do it," Tommy said. "We'll never get in.
There are people everywhere."

Luke said nothing as he watched the movement of a
group of emergency workers inspecting a sandbag levee that
had been built across the entrance to the library's loading
dock. Seemingly satisfied, the group moved on, disappearing
around the side of the building.

"The loading dock," Luke said after a while. "That's our way in. Easy as, bro."

They were crouched among some trees in a small park just across a narrow road from the library's main entrance. The loading dock was on the other side of the road, nearer to the river. Most of the emergency workers were congregated to their right, over on Madison Street.

"Just move slowly," Tommy said. "We'll be hard to see in these dark raincoats, but movement attracts attention."

They advanced carefully toward the river, away from the flashing lights, and crossed the road, skirting along the railway line and heading for the loading dock.

A long ramp that led down into the underground dock was blocked off with the sandbag wall, but they bypassed it, climbing over the side and onto the ramp.

Water gushed around Luke's feet, pouring over the edges of the ramp and flowing down into the loading dock.

Lights appeared along the narrow road, and they both dived down behind the sandbag wall, flattening their backs against it, not worrying about the water that now flowed all around them.

A conversation sounded above, indistinct through the rain, and flashlights played down into the cellarlike loading dock.

Luke held his breath, and after a moment, the lights moved on.

"Let's go," he said, and got to his feet.

His sneakers skidded on the wet ramp and slid out from under him. He hurtled down the steep ramp into the water as if on a waterslide at an amusement park, emerging, cough-ing and spluttering, in the slowly filling swimming pool that was the loading dock.

Luke just had time to call out, "Watch the ramp, it's slipp—" when Tommy landed right on top of him, pushing him back down under the water.

Luke came up choking, spraying water out of his nose, grateful that it was clean rainwater they were in, not the scungy stuff that was flowing down the river.

Tommy popped up next to him and spat out a mouthful of water.

"Are you okay?" Luke asked.

"I was already soaking wet," Tommy said. "Couldn't get any wetter! At least this stuff doesn't smell so bad."

"I think it's rainwater," Luke said. "The drains must be blocked."

A wobbly wooden step led up from the loading dock to a concrete platform where there was a door set into the wall. Luke tried the door.

"It's locked," he said.

"What did you expect? A red carpet and Hawaiian danc-ing girls?" Tommy asked.

"Would've been nice," Luke said.

Tommy opened a waterproof backpack, taking out a small gun-shaped gadget.

Luke watched in amazement as Tommy inserted the thin probe at the end of the object into the keyhole of the door and squeezed the trigger. He turned the handle and the door opened. Easy as.

"It's a lock pick," Tommy explained. "It's what locksmiths use to open doors when people have lost their keys. I bought it off the Internet."

"Don't you have to have a license to own one of those?" Luke asked.

"Yup."

"So, do you have a license?"

"Nope," Tommy said, and handed Luke another item out of his bag of tricks. A tiny pen-shaped flashlight.

Luke followed him into the building and pulled the door shut behind them.

They were back in the corridor that ran beneath the library. If it had been strange and mysterious by day, with the lights on, the corridor was eerie and unsettling in the dark, with just the pencil beams of their flashlights for illumination. Spidery shadows chased each other behind strange objects on the ceilings and the walls, scuttling away from their lights as they played them around the long underground tunnel. Shapes on the walls seemed to reach out toward them as they passed.

Luke had an uncomfortable feeling that they were not alone down here. Maybe it was the spirits of the thousands of dead authors whose books were buried in these subterranean vaults.

The overhead conveyor belt system that had been fascinating to him that afternoon now seemed like some infernal engine, a contraption of torture and evil.

There was a slushing noise as they walked in water that was about two inches deep.

The walls and the ceiling seemed to be closing in on Luke. He looked at Tommy, who appeared to be enjoying himself in this creepy cave, and tried to shake the feeling off. At least the smell of the river was mostly gone, washed from their clothes by their bath in the loading dock.

They passed the storage rooms, their doors sheathed in plastic and sandbagged against the coming flood. At the far end of the corridor, they came to a set of double doors that swung open easily and led to the narrow staircase back to the library's main entrance. They crept to the top of the stairs and looked out through the big glass doors of the entrance.

More flashing lights intermittently gave the library's interior a devilish glow. Luke watched for a moment to make sure that nobody was looking in before scurrying across to the main stairs, Tommy behind him.

"Luke," Tommy said quietly, and Luke turned to see what the problem was. Even in the low strobing light inside the library, their footprints were clearly visible across the gray carpet of the floor.

"It's just water," Luke said. "It'll dry before anyone comes in here tomorrow."

"You sure?"

Luke wasn't but said he was.

There were books stacked everywhere upstairs, safe from the reach of the floodwaters. They sat in piles, with large handwritten labels giving the unit and shelf number they had been taken from.

Luke cast his light around. There were books everywhere. It could take all night to find the one they were after. "This is going to take forever," he said.

"No, it won't," Tommy said. "You said you saw the book just before we were evacuated. That means it will be in one of the last piles. All we have to do is figure out where they finished stacking, and work backward from there."

Luke looked around. It seemed that they had started stacking deep in the interior of the library and finished at the entrance.

"Okay, let's start at this end," he said. "I'll take the left; you take the right."

Tommy nodded and moved toward a stack of books.

Luke dried his hands by rubbing them on the carpet, then began with the nearest pile and scanned the spines. Some of them were blank, which didn't help, so he moved the books off one by one, stacking them neatly so he could replace them later in the right order.

He went through five stacks in that manner and was starting to wonder if he had dreamed seeing the book when Tommy asked, "This it?"

Luke was squatting down. He spun around in excitement, losing his balance and reaching out to steady himself with a hand on the wall.

It *was* it.

It was definitely the book he had seen in the bucket brigade. The picture of the *Vitruvian Man* leaped out at him from the old gray cloth cover, just as he had remembered it.

The words above it were brown and faded, so much so that they were almost impossible to read until Tommy shone his flashlight on them.

Leonardo's River.

Luke's heart seemed to stop for a second. It really was it. The two-million-dollar book. The most boring book in the world.

Tommy handed it to him, and he ran his fingers over the picture on the cover.

"That's the one," he said.

There was a sudden loud crash, echoing around over the sound of the rain.

"What was that?" Tommy asked.

Luke thought he might have heard footsteps. Somewhere *inside* the library.

"Give me your bag," he said.

He stashed the book inside Tommy's waterproof backpack, in among a bunch of gadgets, and sealed the top.

There were voices now, coming up the stairs from the lower level. He could hear them indistinctly but enough to recognize that the language being spoken wasn't English.

"Let's get out of here," he said to Tommy.

They ran as silently as they could into the interior of the library, away from the voices, flicking off their flashlights as they went.

Luke glanced back as two dark shapes appeared at the top of the stairs. He grabbed Tommy's coat and pulled him flat against the wall. "Don't move," Luke hissed.

Two men, large and bulky, were silhouetted in scarlet by the lights coming in from outside. Another man appeared behind them, moving more slowly.

The men all had flashlights, too, but the beams from theirs were an eerie blue.

"Is there another way out?" Luke whispered.

"There's another level above us," Tommy said. "And stairs at each end of the corridor. We could use the back stairs, go along the top corridor, and sneak down the main stairs behind them."

The men were still on the landing, but if they moved farther into the building, Tommy's plan could work.

They were shining their strange lights over the piles of books. Then, just like Luke and Tommy, they set to work; however, unlike Luke and Tommy, they just discarded the books into jumbles on the floor, kicking over piles and searching through the debris. It was clear they were looking for something, but Luke couldn't quite believe they might have been after the same book. Nobody else knew about it.

Then it struck him.

Nobody except a couple hundred people in the human chain that had rescued the books from the basement.

If just one other person in that line knew the story of *Leonardo's River*, then that might well explain the heavies making a mess at the end of the corridor.

Luke realized the men were working their way toward them. "We'd better move," he said, pulling slowly away from the wall.

It wasn't slowly enough.

There was a sudden shout from the group of dark, silhouetted men, and first one, then three blue lights were aimed at Luke.

One of the men pointed a dark shape toward them—a dark shape that looked a little like a gun.

"Run!" Luke shouted, but Tommy needed no urging.

They ran down the corridor through the center of the library, using their flashlights just enough to avoid tripping.

Behind them, Luke heard shouts in a language he didn't understand.

"Hinterher!"

"Wer sind sie?"

"Bringt sie her!"

"This way," Tommy whispered, and turned left through a set of double doors toward another flight of stairs.

They went up two steps at a time, clutching at the handrail to keep from tripping.

Thundering footsteps sounded behind them.

"In welche Richtung?"

"Nach links!"

They reached the top of the stairs. Luke grabbed a thick encyclopedia off a nearby shelf and jammed it into the twin handles of the doors just as the two big men appeared at the glass.

Their pursuers slammed into the door, and the encyclopedia jolted and almost slipped.

It held, but it wouldn't for long.

Luke and Tommy sprinted along the corridor.

Luke heard the doors burst open behind him as they reached the main staircase and hurtled down, two or three stairs at a time. As they approached the main landing, though, he realized they were not alone. One of the men, the oldest one, had remained behind.

Luke's flashlight flicked up and caught his face. It was

not a face you could forget. He was bald, his forehead low and flat, his nose and jaw protruding, and his eyes deep black pools. It was a face to give small children nightmares. It was the face of a vicious attack dog.

The man grabbed Tommy's backpack as he tried to dodge past, hauling him to a stop.

Luke was a few paces behind and didn't even think; he just dropped a shoulder and barreled straight into the man.

If Dog-Face had been younger or sturdier, it wouldn't have worked, but as it was, Luke's shoulder rammed right below his rib cage, bursting all the air from his lungs in a harsh bark, and he fell backward, arms flailing.

"Come on!" Luke yelled, and leaped down, three stairs at a time, Tommy right behind him.

They hit the main entrance and spun around toward the basement stairs. Down the first flight and onto the small landing, and there Luke stopped.

The stairs to the basement were gone.

He was looking straight into a murky well of water.

Not far behind them, Luke heard running footsteps.

"Go!" Tommy said, and without further thought, Luke dived headfirst into the dark water.

9. UNDERWATER

Luke felt strangely safe, despite the darkness and the grip of the water. Surely the men would not follow them. Not down here.

Tommy tapped Luke on the shoulder, but Luke could not see him. Tommy was just inches away but the gloom underground, underwater, was absolute.

Luke remembered the double doors and kicked in that direction, reaching out every few seconds to make sure Tommy was with him.

The pressure in Luke's chest became an ache as they pulled their way through the doors and into the long corridor. Once there, he pushed up to the surface, knowing that if the corridor was completely flooded, then they were in real trouble.

It wasn't. The water was flowing just underneath the ceiling-mounted conveyor belt. He clung on to it and felt Tommy latch on beside him. There was only a few inches of air left, and if the water was still rising, then they didn't have long. He didn't need to tell Tommy to hurry.

Luke pulled himself down the corridor in the pitch blackness, his face upturned in the precious little air that remained. The corridor seemed long enough by day. In the dark, in the water, it was an endurance test. Luke's shoulders began to ache after the first twenty yards and were screaming fire after the second.

He shook off feelings of claustrophobia, knowing that if he let it get to him, he might start to panic. *Hand over hand,* he told himself. *One more foot and then another.*

The air supply remained constant for now, a long, narrow bubble against the ceiling.

It seemed to take forever but it was probably no more than ten minutes before his head cracked into a solid object. They had reached the end.

He felt around and found the doorway through which they had entered. Taking another huge gulp of air, he pulled himself down and through.

A moment later he emerged, puffing and panting, spitting out water, back in the high concrete walls of the loading dock.

Tommy popped up beside him, coughing and treading water. "That was awesome, dude!"

"Are you insane?"

Tommy grinned. "Who were those guys?"

"Buggered if I know, mate," Luke said. "Was that German they were speaking?"

"Yes," he said immediately. "It was German."

"What were they saying?" Luke asked.

"Just stuff like 'this way, that way, chase them,'" Tommy said.

"We'd better get out of here," Luke said. "In case they come outside looking for us."

He didn't think that was likely, considering all the police and the emergency workers around, but he didn't want to take any chances.

The more he thought about it, the more he was sure that the dark object he had seen in the man's hand had been a gun.

10. BLACK FRIDAY

The floodwaters crested that night, Friday the thirteenth, and the town that had been Luke's home for the last three months became a lake.

The river sneered at the pathetic attempts to hold it back with rows of sandbags and plastic, spewing over or around them. The floodwaters did not simply flow and settle over the town; they rampaged in a torrent through the streets, dragging slime and debris through buildings as if they were an open sewer.

The president turned up the next Thursday, as the floodwaters were receding. He rolled up his sleeves and looked as though he was ready to jump on the end of a shovel and start helping with the cleanup, although of course he didn't.

Because of the flood, many roads were closed. The last week of school for the year was canceled, which was lucky, since Luke and Tommy never had to report back to Mr.

Kerr about the book. Luke hoped that by the end of the summer vacation, the fuss about the statue would have died down.

But because the school was closed, nobody knew that Ms. Sheck had been kidnapped for almost a week.

PART II

THE DETECTIVES

The knowledge of all things is possible.
—Leonardo da Vinci

11. GODZILLA THE SQUIRREL

"Something about this book don't smell right," Tommy said.

Luke nodded his agreement as he removed the book from its hiding place, shook off dust and ashes into his garden, and slowly unwrapped the plastic liner that protected it. Even if it was worth a couple million bucks, that still didn't explain the German-speaking thugs in the library, or the gun.

There was more to this book than met the eye, he was sure. Perhaps some long-lost document was sewn into the binding.

He had hidden the book in their ash dump. It was outside the house at the back of the living room chimney, where they emptied the old ashes from their fireplace. It seemed like a nice, safe place for it. It was dry, his house was well outside of the flood area, nobody would use the fireplace until next winter, and who would think of looking there? To be extra safe, he had covered the plastic bag with a layer of old, crumbly ashes.

Nobody knew it was there except Luke, Tommy, and Godzilla the squirrel.

Godzilla sat on a branch of the oak tree by the corner of the house and watched them as Luke unwrapped the book. He was huge. By Luke's reckoning, he was at least half as big again as any other squirrel he had ever seen. He hadn't seen many, as there were no squirrels in New Zealand. With the exception of the drunken squirrel that ruined their prank, Luke thought squirrels were kind of cute, with their bright little eyes and bushy tails. They were usually shy, timid creatures, but you could walk right up to Godzilla while he was sitting there chewing on a nut, and he'd just stare at you and offer you a bite.

Godzilla's head twitched as he watched them walk back inside with the book, as if he were listening to their conversation. But Luke wasn't worried. Who was going to listen to an oversized squirrel?

The floodwaters had come and gone, and so had the president.

Tommy and Luke had talked about little else over the last week except the mad chase through the library and the men who had tried to attack them.

"What could be so important that they'd break into the library in the middle of the night to steal it?" Tommy wondered.

"We did it, too," Luke pointed out. "But what I can't stop thinking about is how quickly they got there. We saw that book about four o'clock, give or take, and less than six hours later, armed thugs were searching the library."

"How did they even know about the book?" Tommy asked.

"There must have been someone else in the line who recognized it," Luke said. "Tipped them off." He stared at the book in his hands. It didn't look like it was worth all the fuss. It just looked like an old, dusty book. "What are you hiding?" he asked the book.

They had spent hours during the week examining the book, looking for clues. They had even scanned it with one of Tommy's gadgets, an ultraviolet scanner, but if there were any clues there, they hadn't found them.

The encyclopedia had been right, though, about its being the most boring book in the world. It was totally unreadable. Luke tried reading it, but after less than a page, he went cross-eyed and his mind wandered. *The Last of the Mohicans* was sounding better and better by the minute. Except he couldn't shake the idea that this book was a clue to some vast mystery.

Both of them pored over the book again, even turning it upside down and trying to read it backward.

Tommy had the idea of x-raying the book to see if there was anything hidden in the binding. He knew someone at the university who might be able to help. Luke liked the idea but thought they had to be careful. The fewer people who knew about the book, the better.

"Maybe we should tell the police," Tommy said after a while. "This whole thing is getting a bit serious for us to deal with."

"Yeah." Luke nodded, but then shook his head. "But how are we going to explain what we were doing in the library? And if they find out we stole the book, then we'll be up to our ears in it." That thought terrified Luke. But so did the thugs from the library. He said, "And what if Dog-Face catches up with us? If they were there looking for the book and couldn't find it, they'll probably assume that we have it."

"You think Dog-Face knows who we are?" Tommy asked.

"I hope not," Luke said.

"And if they do?"

"We'll worry about that then," Luke said, and looked Tommy straight in the eye. "Let's not do anything in a hurry. I gotta be careful. My dad's on a working visa in the States because of his job at the university. If I get arrested, they'll cancel that visa and we'll all be on the next plane home."

He didn't go into details with Tommy, because it was a family matter, but after they'd been forced to sell the farm, his father had scraped by on casual farm labor work, which was both exhausting and humiliating for him.

Then the job had come up at the University of Iowa, with free housing, free private schooling for Luke, and all travel expenses paid. It had seemed like a dream come true, and so far it had been.

Luke just hoped it wasn't about to turn into a nightmare. All because of a stupid, harebrained decision.

Why did he always have to do things like that?

12. VACATION

The first day of summer vacation, Saturday, was strange. Not just because Americans called their holidays vacations or because summer was in the middle of the year. And not because they had already had a week off school because of the flood.

Brown putrid water still covered the town. Most of the businesses were closed, and a lot of roads remained blocked off. You couldn't go visit your friends or go to the movies or to the Coral Ridge Mall. You couldn't do any of the things that Luke had been looking forward to in his first-ever U.S. summer vacation.

It was strange to be stuck at home on the first day of vacation, but it wasn't a disaster.

The second day of summer vacation, Sunday, was a disaster.

Bryan Brown, the son of the principal, was in their class, and he was the first one with the news. "Ms. Sheck is missing," he posted on Facebook. His dad had rung all his staff to see if they had been affected by the flooding and to check that they were okay.

Ms. Sheck hadn't answered her home phone or her cell, so Mr. Brown had driven around to her house. He discovered that the house had been ransacked, and Ms. Sheck was gone.

Luke had heard all kinds of stories from texts and chats—that Ms. Sheck had been arrested, that she'd been murdered, that her entire house had disappeared into the flooded river. But he hadn't heard anything official, and it wasn't until the next day, when it was all over the front page of the local newspaper, that he had any idea what was really going on.

LOCAL SCHOOLTEACHER ABDUCTED, the headline shouted at him. It continued in smaller letters on the next line: EVIDENCE OF VIOLENT STRUGGLE AT HOUSE.

"Holy crap, dude!" Tommy said on the other end of Luke's cell phone. "Do you think it has anything to do with the book?"

"How could it?" Luke asked. "She wasn't even there."

"It does seem strange," Tommy said.

"It's just a coincidence," Luke said. "We saw some strangers in the library when we weren't supposed to be there, and they chased us away. What has that got to do with Ms. Sheck? She probably got in a fight with her boyfriend or owed money to the Mafia in Las Vegas. Why get ourselves in trouble for nothing?"

"I suppose," Tommy said.

"Let the police worry about Ms. Sheck," Luke said.

"What we need to worry about is this book. Who wants it so badly, and why? We need to do some digging around."

That perked Tommy up immediately. "Yeah, dude," he said. "That'd be awesome! We can try out my new laser."

"Bro, it's not space aliens we're up against," Luke said. "At least I don't think so."

13. THE LIBRARY

Gradually, the waters began to recede and the summer rains washed the putrid slime into the drains, clearing away a lot of the sewer smell that had hung over the city.

By Friday, many of the roads had reopened.

The best place to start "digging around" seemed like the university library. That was where everything had happened. And they didn't have anywhere else to start, so they cycled over there from Luke's house, making only a slight detour to Tommy's place to pick up a few gadgets.

Tommy stuffed a few electronic things in his backpack and said he'd explain later what they did.

The police had been at the library.

The doors were open, but yellow plastic tape saying POLICE LINE: DO NOT CROSS blocked off the stairways to the second level. The same tape blocked the stairs down to the basement while cleanup crews and health inspectors made it safe.

From the first level, Luke could see piles of overturned books scattered haphazardly up against the railings. An avalanche of books tumbled halfway down the staircase, reaching almost to the landing.

A fine white powder covered the handrails and walls.

"The police have been dusting for fingerprints," Tommy said quietly beside him. "Do you think we left any?"

Luke thought about that for a moment. "Nah. The only things we touched were the books, and hundreds of people touched those in the bucket brigade."

"They wouldn't have our fingerprints on record anyway," Tommy said with a sigh of relief. "So I think we're safe."

They'd have mine, Luke thought, but didn't say so. In order to get their visa, his whole family had been fingerprinted at the U.S. consulate in New Zealand. And then again at immigration in Los Angeles. He tried to think of anything he might have touched in the library but could think of nothing that wouldn't have been touched by thousands of library users.

"Luke." A cheerful voice came from behind him, and he jumped. It was Claudia. "And I've forgotten your friend's name."

"Tommy," Luke said, turning around to face her.

"I'd like you to meet someone," she said brightly. "This is Mr. James Mullins from New York. He's a book enthusiast and has his own wonderful collection of rare books. He heard about the fantastic job you all did rescuing the collection from the basement before the flood and came down here personally to thank everyone. As it was your idea for the bucket brigade, I thought he'd especially like to meet you."

Luke knew the name, and he knew the face, but he forced his own face to remain calm.

James Mullins was the name of the man who had once offered two million dollars for a copy of *Leonardo's River*. You couldn't forget something like that. Nor could you ever forget his face. The protruding jaw and the snoutlike nose. The deep-set black eyes and the ears that seemed impossibly high on the sides of his head and unnaturally pointed. James Mullins was Dog-Face.

"Hello, Luke," he said. "I hear you did a wonderful job last week. Many of these books are irreplaceable, and it's thanks to people like you that they were saved." He held out a bony paw for Luke to shake.

Luke took it, conscious of his breathing. "Yeah, no worries," he said. "It was my pleasure to help."

"You too, Tommy," Mullins said, shaking his hand also. "A job well done."

"You bet," Tommy said with an embarrassed smile. He didn't seem too concerned about Mullins, and Luke remembered that Tommy hadn't seen Mullins's face that night in the library.

"What happened upstairs?" Luke asked. "What's with all the police?"

Claudia shook her head and shuddered a little as if she couldn't possibly believe that anyone could treat treasured books so cruelly. "Vandals," she said. "Can you believe it? Someone broke in here during the floods and trashed our rare book collection—the books we carried upstairs! Fortunately, there's not much damage, but it's going to take us a long time to get all the books sorted into the right piles so they can be put back in the storerooms."

"Let us know if we can help," Luke said.

"Thank you, Luke," she said. "But it's really a job for the librarians now. A big job, too."

Claudia and Mullins excused themselves and went off to meet someone else. Luke watched them walk away.

"Why are you looking at him like that?" Tommy asked.

Luke told him.

14. A LEAD

"They're up on the second level," Tommy said, "having a look at the damage." His eyes were glued to a pair of miniature binoculars.

"That's a joke," Luke said. "He *caused* the damage."

They were on the second floor of the communications center, across the road from the library, peering in through the windows of the library.

"Okay, now they're heading back down to the first floor," Tommy said. "I've lost them behind the wall—no, wait, they're coming down the bottom of the stairs."

A thought struck Luke and he said, "You don't reckon Claudia Smith is involved in this, do you?"

"The librarian lady?" Tommy said. "Can't see why."

"What are they doing now?" Luke asked.

"He's shaking her hand—looks like he's getting ready to leave."

"Let's go," Luke said. "Try and follow him, find out what he's up to."

They raced down the stairs and were on their bikes on the street as Mullins emerged. They acted casual and were careful to keep a parked car between them and the library.

Mullins got into the backseat of a large silver car, which immediately signaled and pulled out.

Luke and Tommy took off after them.

Iowa City is actually a small town, especially the downtown area, which is arranged in neat rectangular blocks with lots of traffic lights. Tommy knew all the shortcuts and the alleyways and the diagonal pathways that cut across the city blocks, so Luke was pretty sure they could keep up with the car, unless it got on a highway and headed out of town.

The car stopped at the intersection of East Washington Street and indicated a right turn, toward the city center. Luke and Tommy cut up the sidewalk opposite the library and arrived on Capitol Street, outside the Old Capitol Town Center, before the car arrived at the lights. The car went straight ahead.

"We'll have to race around the back way," Tommy yelled, taking off in that direction.

"No time," Luke shouted back. "Let's go through the mall!"

"You can't ride . . . ," Tommy started, then gave up and followed him.

Luke skidded up to the automatic doors to the mall, and they slid open. Then he stamped on the pedals and shot through into the main thoroughfare.

There were people everywhere, but Luke didn't care. He was in a hurry.

Shoppers jumped out of their way as they raced right

through the center of the mall. One lady screamed, although they were nowhere near her at the time.

A man standing at the pizza counter, a big tray of pizza slices in his hands, turned right into Luke's path. He spun out of Luke's way just in time, the tray flipping and the slices of pizza flying into the air. Luke looked back to see him manage to catch the pizza slices with the tray as they started to drop—all except one slice, which flew toward a couple sharing a romantic moment at one of the food court tables. They leaned toward each other, and the girl closed her eyes for a kiss, but instead she got a face full of super supreme.

A beefy security guard patrolling the far side of the mall saw them coming and moved directly into Luke's path, holding up his hands to grab him as he neared.

Luke dodged past a lady drinking from a large plastic water bottle and snatched it out of her hands. He hurled it at the security guard, shouting, "Catch!"

The guard caught the bottle, then watched helplessly as Tommy and Luke sped past him to the doors on the far side of the mall.

A college student holding a Starbucks cup was opening one of the automatic doors. He saw them coming and whipped out of the way with a huge grin and a whoop of excitement.

They shot out onto Clinton Street just in time to see the car turn right, heading straight for them. Luke ducked his head and did his best to lose himself in a crowd of pedestrians until the car had driven past them and turned onto East Burlington Street.

"This way!" Tommy cried, and sped off into an alleyway, pedaling furiously.

Workers were unloading cardboard boxes from a van in the alleyway, but there was just enough room to slip past, with only a slight scrape of Luke's handgrip against the brick wall of the alley.

The silver car passed in front of them as they neared the end, and Luke slid to a halt alongside Tommy at the mouth of the alley.

The car pulled into the loading zone outside the Central Hotel and stopped. A large, bulky man got out of the passenger's side and trotted into the hotel. Mullins stayed in the car.

Luke and Tommy waited, watching, trying to keep out of sight. Eventually, the man emerged from the hotel and got back into the car, which accelerated smoothly away and caught the next green light, turning left.

"Through the hotel!" Tommy yelled. They headed straight for the automatic doors of the hotel lobby, which opened to let them through. They went right in front of the startled reception staff and out through the automatic doors at the other end.

The silver car shot past the end of the pedestrian mall as they emerged, heading north on Linn Street. They took off down Dubuque, through the water fountain, surprising a group of students who were sitting in the lotus position with their hands, palms upward, on their knees.

Ducking and diving through pathways and alleys, they managed to keep up with the car for about five minutes but lost it as it sped through a couple of green traffic lights along Gilbert Street. It didn't matter, though, because by that time Luke had a good idea where it was going. They took a short-cut through Fairchild, and when they pulled onto Dodge Street, he knew that he was right.

The silver car was sitting outside a house.

An old three-story creepy *Psycho* house.

Luke's house.

15. THE GIFT

They waited for Mullins to leave, unsure whether to call the police.

After a while, Luke's mother came out with Mullins, smiling. She shook his hand, and he kissed her on the cheek, which made Luke shudder. She waved as the car pulled away.

"Shall we follow him?" Tommy asked.

Luke shook his head. The car was already almost out of sight, turning the corner. "We know where he's staying now," he said. "We can pick up the trail there later. I want to get home and find out what's going on."

"Oh, there you are," his mother said as they ran up the steps to the front door. "You just missed Mr. Mullins."

"Really?" Luke said. "We met him earlier at the library. What did he want?"

"He left you this," his mother said, handing him an envelope with the Central Hotel logo on it. "He said it was a reward for your actions. Said you had helped save the library or something like that. You never told us anything about that!"

Luke shrugged. "There wasn't much to tell, and there were a lot of people helping, not just us."

He opened the envelope. Inside was a crisp one-hundred-dollar bill. He would have been excited if he hadn't known the truth about the generous Mr. Mullins.

"What about Tommy? He helped, too."

"Yes, yes," his mother said, "I expect there will be a little surprise for you when you get home as well, Tommy. I gave him your address."

Tommy and Luke looked at each other in horror.

"What's the matter, boys?" his mother asked. "You don't seem very excited."

16. DETECTIVE WORK

Iowa City is full of libraries. The university libraries, the public library, the medical library, the hospital library, the science library, and on it goes.

Libraries are full of books.

And books are full of clues, if you know where to look.

Luke didn't, but Tommy did, although he had to do some convincing.

"I hate reading," Luke said, shaking his head. "I'd rather be outside doing something useful."

They had ridden straight from Luke's house to the public library in the pedestrian mall.

"Dude, get over yourself," Tommy said. "Mullins is up to something, and it has to do with that book. We need information, and the best place to start is right here."

Luke looked up at the sandstone-colored walls of the library. The main doors glowered at him like the entrance to a dark, creepy cave full of dangerous creatures.

"How 'bout I go and stake out the hotel," he said. "You can do the research."

"It would take too long," Tommy said. "We both need to do it."

"Okay, okay," Luke said, still staring at the gaping mouth of the library.

"Don't think of it as reading or research," Tommy said. "It's detective work. We are looking for vital clues. It's Operation Mullins."

When Tommy put it that way, it didn't sound so bad.

"Okay, let's rip into it," Luke said.

Inside, Luke was sure prim-faced librarians wearing long dresses and wire-framed glasses would stare disapprovingly at him, but in fact they were greeted warmly by a college student behind the reception desk who answered a couple of questions from Tommy and pointed them to the second floor.

Up against the wall near the stairs was a wooden stand holding the local and national newspapers. He glanced at it and stopped so suddenly that Tommy banged into him.

"What are you doing?" Tommy muttered, but Luke was too busy reading the *Iowa City Press Citizen*.

Like all small-town newspapers, it reported on everything that might possibly interest the people of the city, from a car accident on Clinton Street to a local councilor's dozing off at a meeting. An article in the bottom right corner of the front page was about the break-in at the library. The police, it seemed, had managed to lift a set of fingerprints from the wall near the vandalized books and were following up on this lead.

Luke remembered touching one of the walls to steady himself and hoped it wasn't his fingerprints they had found. He had a horrible feeling it was.

"I made a list," Tommy said, pulling a small electronic organizer out of his pocket as they walked up the stairs to the second floor. "The book is the key to this whole mystery, right?"

"You're not wrong," Luke agreed.

"So we need to learn as much as possible about the book. How did it get to the library in the first place? Who was this Benfer guy who wrote it? Why does it have the da Vinci picture on the front cover? That kind of stuff."

"Okay."

"And we need to find out what we can about Mullins. Who is he? How did he make all his money? Anything that might be useful."

"Okay," Luke said again. "I'll start with the history of the library, see what turns up."

Tommy said, "I'll research—I mean *investigate*—the *Vitruvian Man*. Then we can compare notes."

It was cool on the second floor of the library, even with the sun pouring in through the high glass windows.

Luke found an empty cubicle, then went to one of the library computer stations. He started by typing in "Franklin Library." That was where *Leonardo's River* was supposed to have been kept. A little while later, he was back at the cubicle with a stack of books in his arms. He set them down and looked at them for a while; then, with a large sigh, he settled down to start reading.

• • •

He caught up with Tommy a couple of hours later.

"You go first," Tommy said, with the look of someone who has really big news to tell.

Luke consulted his scrappy notes. "I looked into the other library first, the Franklin Public Library, where the book was donated to. It opened in 1790 in Franklin, Massachusetts, not far from Boston. It's still a library today."

"Might be worth a visit," Tommy said.

Luke had no idea how Tommy thought they were going to get to Boston. In Luke's experience, flying off to another city was not something you just did on a whim. But Tommy seemed to have no problem with the idea.

"The university library here in Iowa City was established in 1855," Luke continued, "but get this—in 1897 lightning struck a chimney and started a fire, which burned down the library! About twenty-five thousand books were destroyed, along with all the catalogue cards."

"You mean their book records?" Tommy asked.

"Yeah. All the information about all the books."

"So if they did have the book—say they'd borrowed it from Franklin—and it was one of the books that survived the fire . . . ," Tommy said slowly.

"Then they might not know they had it, because the records were destroyed."

"They would have made new records, though," Tommy said.

"Yeah, but in the confusion of the fire and everything, maybe they just missed it."

"I wonder if Franklin still wants it back," Tommy said.

Luke laughed, loudly enough that people looked at him. "It must be the most overdue library book in the world," Luke said.

"And Benfer?" asked Tommy.

"He was Italian. A bit of a nobody, really. Had rich parents and fancied himself as an inventor. But he never invented anything worthwhile. He was really fascinated by the idea of flight, which may be why he was interested in the da Vinci drawings. He spent years trying to invent a flying machine but never succeeded. Now your turn."

"Okay." Tommy got out his organizer and scanned his notes. "Let's start with the *Vitruvian Man*."

"The da Vinci picture," Luke said.

"First of all, his name wasn't da Vinci. It was Leonardo."

"We know that," Luke said. "Leonardo da Vinci."

"Nope," Tommy said. "Apparently, they didn't have last names back in the fifteenth century. They called him Leonardo di ser Piero da Vinci, which basically means 'Leonardo, the son of Piero who comes from Vinci.' Calling him 'da Vinci' would be like calling you 'from New Zealand.' His name was Leonardo, and that's how he signed his paintings."

"Leonardo it is, then," Luke said.

"Here's something weird," Tommy said. "He used to write in reverse, you know, mirror writing, so you'd have to see it in a mirror to read it."

"Some kind of code?" Luke wondered.

"Not a very smart one if all you needed was a mirror," Tommy said. "And he didn't do it all the time. Sometimes he wrote the normal way."

"Why?"

"Nobody really knows."

"What about the nude dude in the circle?" Luke asked.

"A circle and a square," Tommy said. "It's supposed to be some kind of study of the proportions of the human body—you know, how long our arms and legs are in relation to the rest of our body. That kind of stuff. Leonardo's version is full of precise measurements."

"Does that help us?" Luke asked.

"Not really," Tommy said.

He opened a large book with glossy pages filled with illustrations.

"Here are some of Leonardo's inventions."

They pored over them. They looked sketchy and old, but Luke could barely tear his eyes from the pages. Here was a guy who imagined submarines, helicopters, tanks, and other things that weren't to be invented for hundreds of years.

"Look at this one," Tommy said. "Leonardo invented a robot. Dude!"

"He had a good imagination," Luke said. "But does it help us?"

"I don't know," Tommy said. "But one thing I did find out is that he didn't let anyone see his drawings. They didn't find them until the nineteenth century."

"That's when Benfer was doing his inventing!"

"Yup. Leonardo kept his drawings private because he was worried that someone might use them for the wrong reasons."

"Good on him," Luke said.

"Get this. He had a hidden laboratory in a monastery in

Florence, and it was so secret that it stayed hidden for over five hundred years. They just discovered it in 2005!"

"What about Mullins?"

"He is from Germany, as we thought. His real name is Mueller—Erich Mueller. He is a world-famous collector of art and rare books, but that's not how he made his money."

"How did he get rich?"

"Rare-earth magnets."

"Which are?"

Tommy took another book and opened it. "The most powerful permanent magnets in the world. Discovered, or rather invented, in 1925. They're made of an alloy, sintered neodymium, whatever that is. They are incredibly strong but also incredibly brittle."

"And Mullins—I mean, Mueller—made millions from magnets? What did he do, invent the smiley face fridge magnet?"

Tommy shook his head. "Computers. They use neo-dymium magnets for the motors in computer hard drives. Mullins got in early on and got rich during the personal computer revolution back in the 1980s."

Luke stared at the stack of books open in front of them, trying to make sense of it all. From Leonardo da Vinci to computer disks. From America's first library to the *Vitruvian Man*.

Somewhere among all this was the solution to the puzzle. But the harder he stared at the books, trying to find it, the more elusive it became.

17. THE BRIEFCASE

The next phase of the operation was to stake out Mullins's—Mueller's—hotel suite. They had no intention of breaking into it, just observing it from a safe distance.

But plans change.

Tommy, who seemed to know every building in Iowa City, led the way through the library to a back staircase. It was locked, but his handy little lock pick took care of that.

The stairs led up to a heavy metal door that had a sliding bolt on the inside but wasn't locked. It opened out onto the roof of the library.

"Stay low," Tommy said. "We don't want anyone to see us."

They both crouched as they scurried across to the northwest corner of the building, overlooking the pedestrian mall. Diagonally opposite was the Central Hotel.

They sat on the concrete roof in the gap between the two library clocks and looked across at the hotel.

"How will we know what room he's in?" Luke asked as

Tommy removed some equipment from his backpack.

He smiled an evil, lopsided grin. "Just call him. I'll do the rest."

Luke glanced at the device that Tommy had extracted from his bag. It looked like a camera but with a long, thin zoom lens.

"What's that?" he asked.

"It's my new laser audio surveillance system," Tommy said.

"What does it do?"

"You aim it at a glass surface, like a window, and it picks up minute vibrations in the glass and converts them into sound waves. Basically, it picks up any noise inside the room."

He plugged a headset into it and put it on.

"You ring the room, and I'll scan the windows, see if I can hear the phone ringing."

"What do I do if he answers?" Luke asked.

"Hang up."

Luke got the hotel number from the directory service and dialed it.

"Central Hotel, Iowa City," a smooth female voice answered.

"Hello, I'd like to speak to James Mullins," Luke said, disguising his voice with his best imitation of an American accent.

"Just a moment." There was a brief period of recorded music. "Putting you through now."

"It's ringing," Luke said.

Tommy was scanning along each floor of the building, listening intently but shaking his head.

It rang four times and then there was a click, and a gruff male voice said, "Hello?"

Luke pressed the END button on his cell phone. "Did you find him?"

Tommy shook his head. "Ring him back."

Luke pressed REDIAL.

"Central Hotel, Iowa City," said the same smooth voice.

"Hello," Luke said, "I was ringing for James Mullins, but I got cut off."

"Oh, I'm terribly sorry." She sounded a bit embarrassed. "I'll put you through again."

The phone rang just twice this time before it was picked up, but that was enough.

"Got it," Tommy said. "Corner room, level three."

Luke disconnected before the voice even had time to say hello.

"Here," Tommy said, handing Luke his pair of tiny binoculars.

Luke put them to his eyes and adjusted the focus, and the wall of the hotel came into clear view. He counted up three levels and found the corner room.

The window's drapes were pulled almost shut. He could make out figures moving around inside but could not see who they were or what they were doing.

"What are they talking about?" he asked.

"They're speaking in German," Tommy said. "They're discussing the phone calls they just got. One of them sounds a little nervous." He listened intently for a while.

"Anything else?" Luke asked.

"Shush," he said, reminding Luke that they were still in, or at least on, a library.

"No, nothing," he said after a while. "I can hear computer keys. I think someone is using a laptop. There are a couple of voices that I can't make out. They may be in another room."

"No mention of the book?" Luke asked.

"None."

Luke let the binoculars wander to the left. He found himself looking into the hotel corridor. Light was reflecting off the glass, which made it hard to see, but he could just make out the elevators halfway down the passageway.

"Hang on, they're leaving," Tommy said. "Mueller told someone to go and get the car."

"All of them?" Luke asked.

"Not sure," Tommy replied.

Luke watched the corridor as one of the heavyset men emerged from the room and went to wait by the elevators. He disappeared, and a few moments later, the other man appeared in the corridor, followed by Mueller.

"They're leaving," Luke said. "Let's follow them."

"I've got a better idea," Tommy said, holding up his lock pick.

They walked into the hotel lobby as if they owned the place.

"Act like you belong," Tommy had told Luke, "and nobody will question you. That's the first rule of successful spying."

They checked the lobby for any sign of Mueller or his thugs, then took the elevator to the third floor and headed for the corner room.

They passed a service cart covered in towels and sheets and packed with little plastic bottles of shampoo and rolls of toilet paper. A few wire coat hangers hung from a handle on the end of the cart. Beside the cart, a door was propped open, and Luke could hear humming and bustling sounds from within.

The room they wanted was at the very end of the corridor and was number 300, according to the brass numbers stuck to the door. A DO NOT DISTURB sign hung from the handle.

"Crap," Tommy said, staring at the lock.

Set into the top of the handle was a slot for an electronic door key.

"Don't you have a gadget for that?" Luke asked.

"There is one, but it costs five hundred dollars, and I haven't bought it yet. Maybe we can ask the housekeeper," he suggested. "Pretend we've locked ourselves out of our room."

"I'm sure they've heard that one before," Luke said, and looked at the handle closely. "Keep a watch out for me."

He strolled casually back to the service cart and borrowed one of the wire coat hangers, untwisting the neck as he walked back to Tommy. Luke straightened out the coat hanger, leaving just the round hook in the end. At the other end he made a handgrip, twisting the wire around into a right angle. Then he pushed the wire underneath the door, up on the other side, and slid it along where the handle should be. He pulled down, there was a click, and the door sprang open.

"That was awesome, dude," Tommy said in amazement, looking at the bit of bent wire and no doubt thinking about that five-hundred-dollar electronic lock picker.

They slipped quietly into the room and closed the door behind them. There was a closet built into one wall, and a door close to the window opened into a small bathroom.

A table and two chairs were in one corner. On the table sat a hotel service directory, a notepad, and a brown plastic pen. The power cord for a laptop computer ran up onto the table, but there was no sign of the laptop. A double bed was in the center of the room, and a single bed was pushed up against the window. The bedsheets on both were rumpled, as though they had been slept in and the maid had not yet come to make up the room.

An open door led into an adjoining room, 302, in which there were two more beds.

"Luke," Tommy whispered. "If Mumbo and Jumbo sleep in here, and that's Mueller's bed, who sleeps in the bed by the window?"

Luke smiled at Tommy's names for the two thugs. "Maybe there's a fourth man," he whispered back, looking around.

"Then let's not take too long," Tommy said.

They searched in the cupboards, and the drawers, and the closets, but all they found were clothes, socks, and under-wear. Men's and women's.

"Maybe the fourth man is a woman," Luke said.

Mueller's bathroom was tidy, while the thugs' was a mess, with towels lying in the middle of the floor and shaving cream spattered across the mirror.

There were some suitcases stacked in a corner, but they were empty.

Luke even checked the pockets of some jackets hanging

in the closet, in case there were any clues in there, but to no avail.

There were footsteps outside the door. They froze, but they heard a door open on the other side of the corridor.

"Dude, we gotta get out of here," Tommy said.

"One more minute," Luke said, checking his watch. He tried the bathroom cupboards, with no success.

It was Tommy who found it.

"Look at this," he said, pulling out a flat black briefcase from under a bed.

Luke looked at the door, wondering how much time they had left, then turned his attention back to the briefcase. It was locked, but Tommy said briefcases were easy. Still, it took him a couple of minutes of fiddling with some small metal device before eventually popping open each of the two locks.

The briefcase was full of papers, mainly in German, although there were also some letters in English that appeared to be business transactions. There was also a small cardboard box containing business cards, with Mullins's name on them, and at the very bottom of the case was a plain manila folder.

Luke opened it.

There were papers inside, the first having nothing on it except for a strange symbol:

"What's that?" he asked.

"Beats me," Tommy replied.

Inside were diagrams—plans for something, but Luke had no idea what. The titles and descriptions were in German. According to Tommy, it was technical vocabulary that he didn't understand, but even stranger than that, they were all written *backward*. All the words and numbers were mirrored.

"Why would they do that?" Luke wondered.

"Ask Leonardo," Tommy said.

There were about ten pages of plans, and Luke went through them one by one, studying them, holding them up to the mirror on the hotel wall and memorizing the diagrams and numbers.

He was on the last page when they heard voices in the corridor outside.

"Luke!" Tommy hissed.

Luke thrust the folder back into the briefcase, slammed the case shut, and shoved it underneath the bed where they'd found it.

There was a beep from the electronic lock on the door.

Luke pointed toward the adjoining room, 302, and they ran into it just as the door to 300 opened.

Guttural voices, speaking in German, filled the room behind them.

They waited until they heard the door to room 300 click shut before opening the door to the corridor as quietly as they could. They ducked out into the corridor and pulled the door shut behind them. Hearts pounding, they took off down the hall, desperate to get out of there in case Mueller and his thugs noticed anything was different.

It was a huge relief when the elevator doors finally shut behind them.

"What were those plans?" Tommy asked.

"Dunno, bro," Luke said. "But if you lock something in a briefcase and hide it under your bed, then it's not exactly going to be instructions on how you like your morning coffee, is it?"

"No." Tommy looked thoughtful as they exited into the lobby and walked calmly out onto the pedestrian mall.

Luke wondered if he'd remembered to relock the briefcase.

His heart was still racing as they left the front entrance of the hotel. How close had they come to getting caught? Everything in the street seemed extra bright and vivid; every detail burned into his brain with the rush of adrenaline that had not yet subsided.

An elderly woman was approaching the hotel through the mall, past the fountain with its six looping jets of water. She looked a little unsteady—from age, Luke guessed, or possibly the bulging bag of groceries she was carrying.

As she got to the fountain, a guy on a skateboard shot out from behind a crowd of people gathered farther up the mall and raced past, just in front of her. He didn't collide with her—in fact, he missed her by about six feet—but it was close enough to startle her. Her foot slipped on a paving stone, wet with runoff from the fountain. She went down onto one knee, then sprawled over onto her side.

Groceries spilled out into the fountain area.

The skateboarder looked back but didn't stop. Some of the crowd drinking beer outside a bar in the pedestrian mall glanced over, then looked away. Maybe they thought she was drunk. A homeless bag lady. Something like that.

"Come on," Luke said, and ran over to where she lay on her side, clutching at her knee.

"I'm all right," she said in short breaths. "I just slipped."

She wasn't all right, Luke thought, but that seemed like the wrong thing to say, so instead he said, "Happens all the time around here. The fountain makes the pathway slippery."

Tommy and Luke each took an arm and helped her back to her feet. Her groceries had rolled in and around the fountain, so they ducked into the water spray, getting wet but collecting the stray items and packing them back into her bag.

"Thank you, boys," she said with an odd expression when they finished. "You are very kind."

She fumbled in her purse and brought out two ten-dollar bills.

"Not on your life," Luke said firmly, and Tommy shook his head also.

Luke took her arm, and Tommy carried the grocery bag as they helped her into the hotel. She limped a little on her injured leg.

The bellboy looked up as they entered, wet and dripping, and came running over, recognizing the woman. The reception clerk also came out from behind the desk, and they both took over from there, assisting the woman toward the elevator, fussing over her.

Just before the door closed, she glanced back at Luke and Tommy and smiled.

"Tommy," Luke said as they left the hotel, "that's a bit odd, isn't it?"

"What?"

"Those hotel rooms don't have kitchens."

"Not the ones we saw," Tommy agreed.

"So what was she doing with all those groceries?"

18. MEMORY

Luke walked into the university's College of Engineering building and found the reception counter unattended. There was a bell, though, and that eventually brought a gray-haired lady scurrying out from a back room. Her name tag said Laura Crisp.

"Hello, sonny, are you lost?" she asked, getting Luke's back up instantly.

"No," he said. "I need some advice on a project, and I was hoping to speak to one of your professors."

It was Monday. Tommy and Luke had gone in different directions. Tommy had gone back to the public library to look into that strange symbol, and Luke had gone to see if he could find someone who would know what the plans were.

Mrs. Crisp looked doubtful. "They're all very busy people," she said. "I'm not sure they'd have time to help you with a school project."

"I'd only need a couple of minutes," Luke persisted.

"To see if they could help me identify a diagram."

She had that expression people use when they really want to just say no but are trying to be polite.

"Which department?" she asked. "We have lots of departments."

"I don't know," Luke said. "Any, I guess."

"Why don't you phone in and arrange an appointment," she said, finding an easy way out. She scribbled a number on a piece of notepaper. "Go to our website"—she added the URL to the note—"and decide who you think might be the best person to speak to. Then we'll see what we can do."

Luke had the feeling that it would never happen, but he said "Thanks" and took the note.

He backed out through the doors into the corridor and headed for the entrance. The main doors opened just as he was nearing them, and a man with thick glasses, a beard, and an ill-fitting jacket entered.

On a hunch, Luke said, "Excuse me, sir, are you one of the professors or lecturers here?"

The man shook his head, which made his glasses slip down his nose, but he stopped. "Sorry, mate, I'm just a technician." He pushed his glasses back into place and started to walk on.

"You're an Aussie!" Luke said, recognizing the accent.

He stopped again and looked at Luke sideways. "Kiwi?"

"G'day, I'm Luke," Luke said. "My dad works over in the agricultural college."

"I'm Heath, g'day," the man said with a quick grin. "I don't hear that around here very much. Who were you looking for?"

Luke explained about the diagram, without telling him where he had seen it.

"So do you have a copy?" Heath asked.

Luke tapped his head. "In here."

"You memorized the entire diagram?"

Luke just nodded.

Heath shrugged. "I'll find you some paper. Draw it for me and I'll show it to a few of the profs. See if anyone recognizes it. Come with me."

He led the way into his office, which was a tiny room tucked at the end of a long corridor, beside the men's bathroom. He unlocked the door with a swipe card and indicated that Luke should sit.

Heath's desk was covered with notes, thick sheaves of paper, and three-dimensional models of strange things with boxes and balls all interconnecting by small tubes. A sign identified him as HEATH THOMPSON, LABORATORY TECHNICIAN.

Heath fished a few sheets of paper out of a box marked RECYCLING and made enough space on the desk for Luke to draw.

Luke sketched the first page of Mueller's diagram as quickly as he could, the numbers and the long German words flowing easily from the cavernous storeroom of his memory. He put that page down and started on the second, while Heath rustled around in a filing cabinet, then made a phone call, his feet up on his desk.

Luke was just starting on the third page when Heath finished the call and idly picked up the first page of the drawings. His feet slid off the desk with a crash, knocking over a wastepaper basket, which spilled paper and lunch wrappings across the floor. He didn't seem to notice. He grabbed at the second sheet and studied it.

"Is this a joke?" he demanded, looking around the room as if searching for hidden cameras.

"No, sir," Luke said in a voice that was not as steady as before.

"Who put you up to this?" Heath asked, snatching away the third page.

"Nobody, sir," Luke mumbled, wondering what the hell was going on. "You said you might show this to—"

"Where did you get this diagram? Where did you see it?"

Luke thought about that for a second or two. He couldn't exactly tell him that he had broken into a hotel room and opened a locked briefcase. He sat back upright in his chair, looking Heath directly in the eye. "I can't tell you that," he said, "because it would get a friend of mine in trouble."

"Your friend is already in much bigger trouble than he wants to be in," Heath said a little more calmly. "I'm going to have to report this."

"That's fine," Luke said, unsure who he was going to report it to. "What is the diagram of?"

"You know perfectly well," Heath said. "Don't you?"

It seemed he still half suspected that Luke was setting him up for some kind of elaborate practical joke.

"No, sir, I don't," Luke said. "What is it?"

Heath looked at Luke keenly, his eyes magnified so large behind his Coke-bottle glasses that his pupils looked like marbles. "These are the plans for a rudimentary fission device."

Luke shook his head. "Sorry, sir. A rudimentary *what* device?" Luke's memory was freakish but fickle. Some things he could remember easily; some things he couldn't remember at all. But what Heath said next he would remember—in full color, in minute detail—for the rest of his life.

Luke rang Tommy as soon as he got clear of the building, which was only after Heath took his name, address, and phone number and rang Luke's father over at the agricultural college to verify who he was.

Tommy answered immediately. "Dude!" he said. "I've been trying to get hold of you. You're never going to believe what I've found out."

That shut Luke up for a moment, because it was exactly what he had been going to say.

19. WEREWOLVES

*I*n the late summer of 1944, World War II was turning against Germany, with Russian forces closing in from the east, and British and American troops advancing through France.

The Third Reich, the German empire that was supposed to last a thousand years, was being dismantled after little more than a decade, and curtains were soon to be drawn on one of the most violent and bloody episodes in human history.

Heinrich Himmler, the much-feared head of the SS (Schutzstaffel), ordered one of his senior officers, Obergruppenführer Hans-Adolf Prützmann, to set up a secret and elite troop of volunteer forces to operate behind enemy lines. They were to be known as Werwölfe (Werewolves).

About five thousand troops were recruited, mainly from the SS and the Hitlerjugend (Hitler Youth). Their tactics included sabotage, arson, and assassination, and by early 1945, about two hundred recruits were in training at the Hülchrath Castle near Erkelenz, Germany.

Their symbol was the Wolfsangel (German for "wolf's hook").

As the war drew to a close, however, the objectives, and the training of the Werewolves, changed.

They became a terrorist organization, trained to operate in secret after the war was over.

A "National Redoubt" was planned—a heavily fortified and defended base in the Bavarian Alps, from where Hitler said that Nazi Germany would "strike back at one minute past twelve using the most efficient secret weapons yet invented."

A system of bunkers was built underneath a hill in Obersalzberg, near Berchtesgaden.

The concrete- and brick-lined tunnels were sheathed with rubber to protect the occupants from the shock waves of aerial bombing. The entrances were covered by fortified machine-gun positions and anti-aircraft defenses.

In the last few weeks of the war, however, it became clear that there would be no last great stand for Nazi Germany. Himmler dismantled the Werewolf organization, and on April 30, 1945, Adolf Hitler killed himself in a bunker in Berlin.

Luke shut the book with a snap that echoed around the silent library and gave it back to Tommy.

The book had been full of photos and biographies of the top people of Nazi Germany—people such as Himmler,

Göring, and Speer. There were photos of Obersalzberg and their fancy holiday homes, and pictures of the bunkers. There was also a timeline of the events leading to the end of the war.

It was amazing how much you could learn from a book, really.

"Werewolves," Luke said. "You reckon Mueller is a Werewolf?"

"I'm sure of it."

Luke was doubtful. "He'd have been just a kid when the war ended."

Tommy nodded. "Yeah, I thought about that. But the Werewolves were recruited from the Hitler Youth, or maybe he is the son of one of the Werewolves."

"But the book said they were disbanded."

"Maybe they weren't," Tommy said. "Maybe shutting down the Werewolf organization in 1945 was just a cover-up. Maybe they've been hiding out somewhere, waiting for Hitler's 'one minute past twelve.'"

"Hiding for over sixty years, waiting for their chance to strike back," Luke said. "That doesn't figure. Why wait till now?"

Tommy shrugged. "Beats me. Maybe they were waiting for something like a particular date or a certain world event. I don't know."

"It has something to do with the book," Luke said slowly. "*Leonardo's River.* It all seems to hinge on that book."

"How could it?" Tommy asked. "That book was written almost a hundred years *before* World War Two!"

"Dunno, bro," Luke said, "but that book is the key. Mueller

dropped everything to come here and search for that book."

"So what was your news?" Tommy asked.

"These Werewolves," Luke said with a dry mouth. "Mueller and his neo-Nazi terrorists. They've got a nuclear bomb."

20. JUST WALKING

It was one thing to play at being detectives, but there was a point when it all got too much. Too serious.

Luke and Tommy were *way* past that point.

They typed a letter on one of the library computers, detailing everything they knew. The plans for the bomb. The symbol that connected Mullins with the Werewolf organization. The lot. Then they printed it on one of the library laser printers and bought a plain brown envelope from the bookshop in the pedestrian mall.

On the front of the envelope they wrote "URGENT: SENIOR DETECTIVE." That seemed like it would get to someone appropriate. They wrote the letters alternately in block capitals. Luke wrote the *U*, and Tommy wrote the *R*; then Luke wrote the *G*, and so on. They hoped it would confuse the police handwriting experts.

Then Tommy pulled a baseball cap down over his eyes, strolled casually into the police station on Washington Street, and slipped the envelope onto the desk of the officer on duty.

From here on, it was up to the authorities, and he was sure they would know what to do.

Tommy headed home. He was going to spend the evening on the Internet, seeing if there was any more information to be found about Herr Mueller and his friends.

Luke went for a walk.

There seemed to be so many different facts swirling around in his head, like pieces of a jigsaw puzzle, but he just couldn't make them all fit together so he could see the whole picture.

When he needed to think, he walked. It always seemed to clear his head. Just strolling, looking at what was around him, letting his mind idle, instead of stamping on some mental accelerator, trying to force himself to come up with a solution to the problem.

The plans in the briefcase had been mirrored. Leonardo sometimes wrote in mirror writing, too. Was that some kind of connection? What about Mueller's company? He had made a fortune out of rare-earth magnets. Was that important?

The Franklin Library had owned the book but had lost it. The Iowa University Library had the book, but their records had been destroyed in a fire. Could the fire have been deliberate? No, it was started by lightning. What about nice Claudia Smith? She seemed to get on well with Mullins/Mueller. A little too well, maybe? Was she involved somehow?

Images floated through his mind. The *Vitruvian Man*.

The unmade fourth bed in the hotel room. Werewolves. Atomic bombs. Leonardo hiding his laboratory so well it wasn't found for five hundred years, and keeping his drawings secret so they wouldn't be misused.

Ms. Sheck. Missing. Was it possible that she was connected to this in some way?

More images faded in and out: the photos from the history books, Heinrich Himmler (nerdy-looking), Hermann Göring (fat and pompous), Albert Speer (dignified), and the dank concrete tunnels of the underground Nazi bunkers. Photos of the destruction and death of countless millions of people in World War II. Images that he wished he could wash from his mind but that he knew would be with him forever, playing again and again on a permanent loop in his brain.

He walked until the sun dropped below the tall buildings by the river, and the low golden twilight was replaced by deepening shadows. A snake slithered suddenly across his path on Dubuque Street, winding itself into some shrubs as he approached. Luke didn't know who was more startled, him or the snake. There were no snakes in New Zealand.

By the time he got back to his bike, his head was clear. He still didn't know the answers, but he knew what he had to do. He wasn't looking forward to it—he was dreading it, in fact—but he knew it had to be done.

He had to read the book.

The most boring book in the world.

21. THE MOST BORING BOOK

He finished dinner quickly, even though it was his favorite—macaroni and cheese—and he didn't have seconds, which got his mother worried.

"Are you feeling all right, Luke?" she asked as he rinsed his plate in the sink.

"Yeah," he said. "I'm just going to go and do some reading."

His father and mother exchanged glances across the dinner table.

"Reading?" his mother said. "That's a nice change. What are you going to read?"

"The most boring book in the world," Luke said.

His mother sighed. "We talked to Mr. Kerr about this," she said. "It's not really the most boring book in the world."

"Oh, yes, it is," Luke said, and headed up to his room.

When his parents had settled in the living room—his mother reading a magazine and his father going over some lecture notes—Luke snuck back down and made himself a cup of coffee.

He didn't actually like coffee, and his mother disapproved of him drinking the stuff, so he did it quietly, using two teaspoons of instant coffee and sugar but leaving out the milk. Then he tiptoed around outside the house and retrieved the book from its dusty, ashy hiding place.

He sat down at his desk to read, thinking that if he lay on his bed, it would be too comfortable. Too sleep-inducing. As another precaution, he set the alarm on his watch to go off every half hour.

Then he slowly opened the old gray cloth cover of *Leonardo's River*. Fastening his eyes securely on the first word, he began to read.

It was a dark and gloomy afternoon. Not dark like the night, nor light like the day, but something in between like brass, which is not quite copper and not quite zinc. It was the kind of dark that seems to come in waves of gloom and despair. Big waves, small waves. Midsized waves. Waves in between midsized and big, and others in between midsized and small, all crashing together on the tortuous, tormented sea that was the sky, to create a darkness that was gloomy and despairing. Not as despairing as losing a loved one (unless that loved one was a distant relative, or perhaps a former lover for whom your ardor had cooled, and whom you had not seen for a long time, maybe a few years, or even a decade, but certainly longer than a few months. Enough time for the love to fade, because as love fades, so does the despair of losing that loved one fade in concert). Yes, the despairing darkness of the day was great, but not absolute. Enough to sap your enthusiasm and energy, but insufficient to thieve your will to live (unless you were already suffering from depression of the clinical kind, in which case the added weight of the dark and gloomy sky might be enough to tip you over the edge, but probably not, and in any case if you were already of that nature, you should be consulting a doctor who could prescribe a vigorous tonic, or perhaps a holiday in the country to lift you out of your moroseness).

The darkness came from the clouds, which were heavy and sodden. Probably cumulus clouds, which are the puffy, cotton-wool type that seem gentle and often make shapes on warm summer days. They are the friendliest of clouds, except when angry, with rainwater just waiting to be unleashed on the earth, as were these clouds, so full of moisture, in fact, that they were entirely gray, with not a trace of the white cotton wool around the edges that is often seen when the day is not so full of rain.

Cirrus clouds are another common cloud, but more distant and not so friendly, and in any case there were no cirrus clouds around, unless they were high in the sky, hidden from view by the wet darkness of the cumulus clouds below them.

It was dark. It was gloomy. It was the afternoon. A dark and gloomy afternoon.

Luke rested the book on his chest after the first page and rubbed his eyes for a moment.

A whole page, and all the author had said was that it was cloudy. He shook his head in disbelief and turned the page.

Despite the strong black coffee, he fell asleep in chapter two. And again in chapter five. Not to mention chapters six, seven, nine, and thirteen. But each time, the shrill beeping of his watch alarm roused him and he forced his eyes back to the page.

It was a novel but an awful one. Benfer would start off by describing some really unimportant thing in intricate, page-after-page detail, and before he was even finished, he would get sidetracked into something completely irrelevant and then go off on another tangent. Given the choice between this and *The Last of the Mohicans*, he would have happily read the other book seven times over.

In the end, it was chapter fourteen that finally got him. It was after midnight. Luke dozed off for the last time, and no amount of beeping from his watch was going to wake him up.

When he awoke to the sound of his cell phone ringing, it was seven-thirty.

He hadn't finished the book, and he couldn't shake the feeling that he had been on the verge of discovering something.

Something tremendously important.

22. THE VITRUVIAN MEN

It was Tommy on the phone. "Get over here," he said.

"Why?" Luke asked sleepily.

"I'll meet you at the Burlington Street Bridge," he said. "On my side of the river. I'll explain when you get here. Hurry!"

Luke dressed quickly, grabbed his backpack from the closet, and munched a breakfast bar on the way out the door.

Hurry or no hurry, he still took the time to wrap the book in its protective plastic liner and stow it in the ash dump before unlocking his bike from the rack behind the house and heading for the bridge.

It was busy with traffic at this time of the morning and blocked at one point by a pickup truck parked right on the walkway. Cleanup workers wearing plastic gloves and paper face masks were loading smelly gray sandbags onto the truck. Luke had to skirt around them to reach Tommy on the other side.

"What is it?" Luke asked.

Tommy didn't answer but took off along the riverside path. Luke followed, wondering what all the drama was about.

The footpath was muddy in places and still smelled of the floodwaters.

"Remember we thought it was strange that Mueller got here so fast?" Tommy asked.

"Yeah," Luke said, pedaling furiously to keep up with him.

"Well, I found out that he lives in New York. So if that's where he was when he heard about the book, then the only way he could have got here in time was to fly."

"Okay."

"So I checked on his company, the magnet manufacturers, and found out that they have a private jet, a Gulfstream G100."

He stopped talking but kept pedaling, looking at Luke, quite proud of himself, Luke thought, and rightly so. If only Luke had managed to stay awake last night, he might have made some discoveries of his own.

"So I texted Ben Pickering. You don't know him; he's Nick's older brother. He's one of those plane-spotter nuts. He said there was a Gulfstream sitting outside a hangar at the airport. Flew in the night of the flood."

"Didn't they shut down the airport?"

"Nope, it never flooded, so they kept it open, according to Ben."

"I think we should call the police," Luke said, slowing down.

Tommy came to a halt in front of Luke. "And tell them what? We already told them about Mueller and the atomic bomb stuff. Have they done anything about that?"

"I don't know," Luke said.

"If we just tell them that Mueller has a plane at the airport—and we don't even know yet if it is his plane—then they won't do anything. We need some evidence."

Tommy seemed to be getting a little bit carried away with the whole spy thing. When he took off again, Luke followed reluctantly.

The morning was warm, and a mild breeze was at their backs, helping them along.

"I read some of the book last night," Luke said, pulling up alongside Tommy.

"What did you find out?" Tommy asked.

"I'm only about halfway through," Luke said. "It's all about Leonardo and his patron, Cesare Borgia, who was the son of the pope, and some other bloke named Heidenberg—Johann Heidenberg. It's some type of a historical novel, but nothing happens, and it keeps not happening for page after page after page."

"What's a patron?" Tommy asked.

"Kind of like Leonardo's boss, I think," Luke said. "Some rich guy who could pay his wages while he did his work. Something like that."

"Is that all you found out?" Tommy asked.

"Nah, bro," Luke said. "The book goes on for ages about Leonardo's paintings and his inventions, with heaps of details and measurements, but in amongst it there are things that will blow your mind. I dunno if it's true, but if it is, then it's almost unbelievable."

"Such as?"

Luke paused a moment for dramatic effect, then said, "Rare-earth magnets."

Tommy coasted to the left as the path split off from the road, down toward a small wooden bridge. Ahead of them, a rusted railway bridge towered in the air, resting on dirty concrete pillars that were scrawled with graffiti.

Tommy said, "Benfer must have made that up. Rare-earth magnets weren't discovered until centuries after Leonardo died. How could he have known about them?"

Luke had known he was going to ask that. It had been his first thought, too. "Tommy," he said, "think about it. Rare-earth magnets weren't discovered until nearly a hundred years *after* Benfer wrote the book. How could Benfer have known about them? Unless Leonardo really had discovered them hundreds of years earlier."

Tommy shook his head. "But then we'd have known about them since the fifteenth century."

"In the book, Leonardo hushes up the discovery. Keeps them a secret. He thinks they are too powerful ever to be made public."

"Too powerful?" Tommy mused. "You mean powerful like magnetic powerful."

"No, I don't think so," Luke said.

"Do you think that's why Mueller wants the book?" Tommy asked. "Because of the magnet information? He got rich out of rare-earth magnets; there has to be a connection."

"Yeah, but what?" Luke asked. "And you know the nude dude?"

"The *Vitruvian Man*?"

"Yeah. Get this. There's not just one. That picture, according to Benfer, is one of a whole series. They're in the book with measurements and everything."

"Was there anything at all that would help explain what Mueller is up to?" Tommy asked.

"No," Luke said. "Not yet."

Something important was still scratching at the back of his mind, but he would have to do more reading to find out what it was.

The Iowa City Municipal Airport was on the southeast side of the city, on the opposite side of the river from the downtown shopping area. It was a small, general aviation airport with two runways and a number of hangars.

It was a fifteen-minute ride there from the bridge.

They cycled past an old air force jet fighter that was mounted on a tripod. It was on an angle as if it had just taken off, zooming into the sky to do battle with unknown enemies. The road led through a grove of trees to another road, which looped in a big circle in front of the airport building.

"Gotta be careful," Luke said. "If they *are* here, we don't want to be spotted."

"You bet," Tommy said.

They left their bikes on the parking lot side of the airport building, away from the large hangars that stretched out to the left.

Luke stared through a wire mesh fence. A number of light aircraft were parked in neat rows.

"Here," Tommy said, and held out a pair of dark sunglasses for Luke. "We don't want to be recognized."

Tommy looked so serious that Luke almost laughed, but instead he took them and put them on. Tommy put on a matching pair and then handed Luke one of his secret MP3 radios before slinging his own around his neck.

"Can you hear me?" Luke asked into his radio.

"Clear copy, Luke. One, two," Tommy said, and added as an afterthought, "Over."

Luke crept to the edge of the building and peered around. Nobody was in sight. He waited for a moment or two, watching for any sign of movement, then motioned to Tommy. They slipped quietly around the front of the building. The single glass front door of the small terminal appeared to be locked, and no lights were on inside.

"There's a staircase around the other side," Tommy said, "and a viewing platform on the roof."

That sounded like as good a place as any to be, so they moved as stealthily as they could around the far side of the building and up the staircase. It was made of metal, and their footsteps seemed to echo loudly around the deserted airport, but it might just have been Luke's nerves that magnified them.

They crept to the top and lay down on the platform. It was also made of metal, with crisscrossed indentations to make it less slippery. It wasn't that comfortable to lie on, but it gave them a good view of the entire airport.

"There," Tommy said, pointing.

The tail of a small jet plane stuck out from one of the hangars, gleaming orange in the low sun. There were letters, some kind of call sign, on the tail, but it was otherwise unmarked. The underbelly and the lower part of the tail were painted a deep blue.

From their vantage point, they could see right into the hangar, and other than the plane, it seemed to be empty.

Tommy was studying the plane through his dinky miniature binoculars. "That's got to be the one," he said. "Write down the registration number from the tail and we can look it up on the Internet later—see if it is Mueller's plane."

Luke nodded but didn't write the number down. He didn't need to.

A heavy mesh fence cut the tarmac off from the rest of the airfield. It extended to the corner of one of the hangars, blocking all entry to the runways. Another, smaller fence secured the hangars. It was lower, but the top was covered in sharp spikes.

"It's in hangar two," Tommy said. "What do we do?"

"I know what I'm going to do," Luke said. "What's the range of this radio?"

"Long enough," Tommy replied. "The length of a football field at least."

"Okay. I'm going to have a look in the hangar. You were right. We need some kind of evidence. Stay here with the binoculars. Keep a lookout. If you see anyone approaching the airport, or anyone moving around the hangars, let me know."

"Okay." Tommy sounded slightly relieved. "But how are you going to climb the fence?"

"I'm not," Luke said.

There was no need to. The viewing platform stretched out over the terminal building, over the tarmac and the fence.

"Hang on," Tommy said, and scrabbled around in his backpack. He handed Luke a rubberized tube, about a yard long.

Luke shook his head, not understanding.

"It's a periscope," Tommy said, and extended it to more than double its length before collapsing it back. "You can use it to look around corners without being seen."

Luke put it in his backpack; then he handed the backpack to Tommy and climbed up onto the safety rail, swinging one leg over and letting himself down with his arms until he was hanging on by his fingertips over the floor of the platform.

Tommy looked worried, but Luke was confident he could make the jump.

He pushed off to get clear of the window ledges and dropped to the concrete pad outside the terminal, rolling over like a paratrooper to spread the shock. His sunglasses went flying off. He collected them and tucked them into his T-shirt.

Tommy tossed the backpack down to him, and Luke caught it neatly.

"All clear?" he asked.

Tommy's voice came back through the earphones. "Roger that, over."

Luke skirted the mesh fence to the edge of the first building. The huge hangar doors were open, and inside were several aircraft: one was a small jet and the others were propeller aircraft. One of the prop planes had its front hood removed, exposing the engine.

He could see a glass door on the far side of the hangar, so he slipped inside, rather than continue on the wide-open tarmac. He ducked underneath the wing of the jet, crossed the hangar floor, and dodged around the plane with the hood off. It was dim inside, and he kept an eye on the floor for anything that could trip him up and make a noise.

At the far door, he stood against the wall and used Tommy's periscope to examine the next hangar. Hangar two. From this angle, he couldn't see the tail of Mueller's jet.

There was a matching glass door on the wall of hangar two, opposite him.

"You still with me?" he asked.

"Affirmative. Watching you like a hawk," Tommy said in his ears.

Luke clipped the periscope to his belt and opened the door slowly, checking left and right before sprinting across to the door of the next hangar. It was locked.

To his left, across a wide concrete area, another big hangar was jam-packed with equipment, including a military-looking jet, painted yellow and blue.

Luke could see someone moving around behind the jet. Whoever it was disappeared through a door at the back, and Luke slid along the wall to the front of hangar two. He used the periscope to look around inside.

"All clear as far as I can see," Tommy said from his vantage point. "But stay frosty, over."

Luke tucked the periscope away and eased around the corner. It was dark inside, and he waited a moment for his eyes to adjust.

At the rear, a walled-off area created an office, which had windows looking out onto the hangar. On either side of it, staircases led up to a second level with another office.

In the center of the hangar, some unmarked wooden crates were stacked in a pyramid. Each was about the size of a refrigerator lying on its side. Behind them, a large forklift sat silently.

Luke wondered what was in the crates and thought of the chilling plans they had found in Mueller's briefcase.

Feeling a lot more nervous than he hoped he appeared, he strolled into the hangar. Nobody shouted. Nobody saw him. It was deserted.

Luke looked at Mueller's plane—if it was Mueller's plane—and wondered what it would be like to be so rich that you could own a jet. Then he moved closer to the offices at the rear of the hangar. They were dark behind the windows, probably deserted. He tried the handle of the downstairs office door. It was locked.

"All good," Tommy said.

Luke moved around to the left-hand staircase and put his weight carefully on the first step, listening for creaks or groans. It took his weight without complaining, so he cautiously moved upward.

He was halfway up when Tommy's voice came again, this time with urgency.

"Freeze," he said. "Danger close. A light just came on in the top office!"

Luke froze.

"Someone's moving around in there," Tommy said. "Stay where you are."

Luke flattened himself against the back wall of the staircase, knowing that would make no difference if someone emerged onto the landing above him.

"Door just opened! Get out of there!" Tommy shouted.

Luke could see the light spilling out of the doorway above. He turned and ran back down the stairs as quietly as he could and ducked around the front of the downstairs office.

Directly above, he could hear footsteps on the landing.

"It's Jumbo," Tommy said. "He's right above you."

So it *was* Mueller's hangar. Luke forced himself to breathe calmly.

Tommy said, "He's coming down! He's coming down!"

"Which stairs?" Luke whispered.

"Left," Tommy said, adding, "My left."

Luke padded to the right-hand staircase and flattened himself onto it, going up using his hands and feet as Jumbo went down the stairs on the other side. He got to the top and peered over the edge in time to see Jumbo unlock the lower office door and enter.

"Keep an eye on him," Luke whispered.

He grabbed the periscope again and extended it fully, lying flat on the landing and pushing the end of it to the open doorway there. The lens gave him a clear view inside the office, which looked empty.

"I think you should get out of there," Tommy said.

Luke ignored him, getting slowly to his feet and creeping to the door. It was a tiny office, with a sofa at one end, a small sink at the back, and a desk against one wall. From the arrangement of the cushions, it was clear that Jumbo had been sleeping there. *Why?* he wondered. The Central Hotel looked much more comfortable.

He returned to the landing, careful not to make any loud footsteps that would be heard in the room below.

He waited.

Finally Tommy said, "Okay, he's coming out. He's going back up the right stairs."

Luke crept over to the left staircase and let himself down it as Jumbo climbed the other. He had reached the base without incident when Tommy came on the radio again. "A car has just pulled up outside the terminal."

What now? thought Luke.

"I think it's Mumbo."

"What's he doing?" Luke asked.

"Unlocking the gate," Tommy said. "Danger close! Danger close! He's going around the front of hangar one."

Luke looked around desperately. Where could he hide? The boxes? The stairs? There was nowhere he would be hidden from both the front and the back of the hangar.

"He's coming along in front of your hangar now."

Luke ran toward the jet, dropping and sliding underneath the main fuselage as footsteps entered the hangar in front of him.

He wasn't quite hidden, but the shadow of the jet made a dark pool on the hangar floor that swallowed him up.

"Top office door has just opened," Tommy said quietly. "Jumbo's come back out."

Luke listened as Tommy kept up a commentary.

"Mumbo's walking in; he's right alongside you now. Don't move a muscle."

Luke didn't, except for the one twitching in the back of his neck.

"He's looking at the jet. Jumbo's coming down the stairs. They're talking, I think."

They were arguing, but it was all in German, so Luke had no idea what they were saying.

"Mumbo's giving Jumbo the car keys," Tommy said. "It seems like a sort of changing of the guard."

Changing of the guard meant there was something *to guard*, didn't it?

"Mumbo's going into the lower office, and Jumbo's heading out, back to the car, I think. . . . Okay, you're clear. No, wait—I can see Mumbo moving around. Stay where you are."

There was a muffled noise from above. Luke looked up sharply at the underbelly of the plane that was hiding him.

Keeping on the side of the craft that was away from the offices, he rolled out from beneath the jet and stood up. Luke pushed the periscope up the side of the plane to one of the oval windows. The cabin appeared to be empty. He moved forward as far as he could, but the wing was blocking his way, so he crept closer to the front of the plane and stretched the periscope out to one of the other windows.

He put his eye back to the lens and couldn't see anything for a moment. Something was blocking his vision. He thought it might be the shade and tried to move the periscope for a better look, but the thing suddenly moved, twisting around toward him.

It was a person.

For a fraction of a second, his mind wanted to tell him that it was Mueller, staring straight at him. But it wasn't.

Mueller didn't have wild blond hair.

Mueller didn't wear black eyeliner.

Mueller didn't have a silver stud in the side of his nose.

It was Ms. Sheck.

"Ms. Sheck's here," Luke whispered. "She's in the jet."

She didn't seem to notice the narrow tube of the periscope outside the window.

"You're kidding," Tommy said.

"No, bro, I just looked right at her."

"What the heck is going on?" Tommy asked. He broke off and came back with "Jumbo is driving away, and Mumbo is coming out of the office. Stay frosty, over."

Luke stayed as still as he could. He had an idea. He took his cell phone and held its camera lens to the eyepiece of the periscope. He pressed the camera button two or three times, not knowing if it would work.

"He's going upstairs. He's in the office. Door's open, but I think you're okay."

Luke put the periscope away in the backpack and started toward the hangar door.

He almost made it, too.

23. UNDER ARREST

Luke heard the guttural shout behind him just as Tommy yelled in his ear, "He's seen you! Run!"

A flick of his head, and he saw Mumbo leaping down the stairs from the second-floor office.

Luke ran. He had a small head start but not much. He ran from the hangar as fast as he had ever run in his life. His backpack bounced up and down, the straps cutting into his shoulders. The sunglasses flew from his T-shirt and disappeared somewhere behind him.

"He's at the bottom of the stairs!" Tommy informed him.

The edge of the building flashed past, and he ducked into the gap between the two hangars. The smaller fence around the hangar area would be easier to climb than the larger mesh fence by the terminal building.

"He's out of the hangar!" Tommy yelled.

Luke didn't look back.

He could feel each throb of his heart within the wall of

his chest. His ears drummed with each heartbeat. He cut close to the far corner of the first hangar and hurtled toward the fence. The jagged spikes on top looked vicious. There was a D-shaped hole in the gate where the lock was.

"He's right behind you!" Tommy screamed.

Luke flipped off his backpack as he sprang at the fence, throwing it up on top of the spikes. His foot found the D in the gate, and he launched himself up, scrabbling over the spikes, protected by his backpack. A hand brushed at his ankle, but he was over.

He landed in another paratrooper's roll.

The backpack was caught on the jagged barbs. He left it there.

Tommy was running down the stairs from the walkway and heading for the exit road.

"The bikes!" Luke yelled.

Behind him, Mumbo was fumbling with a key at the gate.

Tommy and Luke darted around the side of the terminal to where they had put the bikes.

They jumped on and raced onto the looping road toward the exit.

Mumbo was through the gate now and running across the grassy center of the road, trying to cut them off. He was going to make it, too. They had too much distance to cover.

"Keep going!" Luke urged Tommy. "Get out of here."

Luke changed direction and bumped up over the curb onto the hard grass circle in the center of the road, heading straight for Mumbo.

Mumbo stopped, confused. If nothing else, that would give Tommy a chance to get away.

He was a big man and solid across the chest, a wrestler or a boxer, maybe. Definitely a thug. He turned to meet Luke, who was speeding straight at him over the bumps in the grass. His big gorilla hands came up to grab the bike as Luke closed in for the head-on collision.

The world seemed to slow. Mumbo's teeth clenched in a grimace as he braced himself for the impact, and a flock of birds rose in unison from the trees behind his head.

Then the unexpected.

Luke gave a sharp twist on the handlebars just as Mumbo got within reach. The bike was no longer upright but was dropping, sliding horizontally right at Mumbo, taking Luke with it. The rear wheel whacked into Mumbo's leg with a crunch that would have broken the ankle of a smaller, weaker man. His legs flipped out from under him, and he fell heavily, landing face-first on the field.

Luke jumped back up and stood on his pedals. His bike shot off the grassy area and back onto the road. He glanced back to see Mumbo get to his feet and start running, only to stop as his ankle collapsed beneath him.

Mumbo reached into a pocket, brought out a cell phone, and pressed it to his ear.

Tommy looked around as Luke turned onto the highway and slowed to let him catch up. "What happened?" he asked, the words coming in gasps.

"He fell over." Luke managed a grin, sucking in the air.

A huge truck thundered past, moving to the left to give

them room. The driver glared at them through the windshield, two kids on bikes going the wrong way down a main road.

"We need to split up," Luke yelled.

"Why?"

"We need to get to the police and tell them about Ms. Sheck. But Mumbo had a cell, so they're going to come looking for us. If we split up, there's a better chance that one of us will get through."

Tommy nodded without looking around. "You take the river path, the way we came. I'll take the back road. I know the roads around here better than you."

"Okay."

Tommy split off at the intersection with the main highway.

Luke didn't wait for the traffic lights to change but just caught a break in the traffic and quickly pedaled through the intersection. He could see the McDonald's on the river side of the road. That marked the first bridge, he remembered, and he cut across the road toward it, bouncing up onto the sidewalk as he crossed over the bridge.

His tires left black marks on the pavement as he scudded around the corner onto South Capitol Street. There was a campus police station by the Old Capitol Town Center, which was much closer than the main station at city hall. He was close now. Close to safety. The black shadow of the railroad overpass slid across him, and he pumped the pedals furiously, beads of sweat breaking from his face and flicking away behind him.

Once he got to the police station, everything would be

okay. They would rescue Ms. Sheck and arrest Mueller, and life would return to normal.

He made it as far as Burlington Street.

At first he didn't realize anything was amiss. He didn't recognize the car, and the windows were tinted, so he couldn't see inside. He should have been suspicious when it passed him and then slowed, even though there was no intersection looming or traffic to give way to.

The car slowed further, and Luke, still pedaling frantically, caught up just as it swerved across his path. A low concrete wall to his right gave him nowhere to go. He yelled and slammed down on his brakes, skidding, sliding, then crunching into the side of the car with a bruising thud.

He tried to get up quickly, but the ground was swaying underneath him and it was hard to balance. Then Jumbo was standing over him.

It might have been the adrenaline, but his strength and his balance came back in a rush, and he rolled away from the man. He sprang to his feet and started to run, until a rough hand on the collar of his shirt jerked him backward and sat him down hard on the sidewalk.

Luke leaped back up and spun around, hands raised, but a huge fist was already coming toward his face. It connected. His head rocked back, and he fell to the ground. He sat up and saw that sledgehammer fist drawing back again. He shut his eyes.

"Hey!" A voice cut through the pain in his face. A voice he recognized, although through the fog in his head he could not place it. "Hey, what are you doing? Leave that boy alone."

The hand on his collar came loose, and the fog over him lifted as his attacker faced the new threat. Luke turned his head to see his savior and his heart sank.

Mr. Kerr, the jelly-doughnut vice principal of his school, was advancing on Jumbo, a set of car keys in one hand and a Taco Bell bag in the other. He caught a glimpse of Luke's face. "Luke? What the hell is go—"

Mr. Kerr didn't get a chance to say another word as he came within range of Jumbo's massive reach.

Jumbo spun up at him, his fist swinging around in a blow that would surely knock Mr. Kerr's fat head clean off his shoulders.

Except that Mr. Kerr's right hand, the one holding the car keys, jerked upward in a block, forcing the punch to the side. In what looked like a reflex action, his other hand shot out in a hard left jab that connected with Jumbo's nose, snapping his head back.

Once upon a time, in some former life, Mr. Kerr had known karate.

The jab alone would hardly have been more than a bee sting to a thickheaded thug like Jumbo, except the hand doing the jabbing was the hand holding the Taco Bell bag, which split, and a container of volcanic chili sauce exploded over Jumbo's face.

Jumbo yelled and wiped at his eyes. He thrust out with a low, double-fisted punch, most of which got absorbed by the rolls of fat on Mr. Kerr's chest, but there was still enough force in it to knock Mr. Kerr over.

Jumbo yelled again, in agony, still pawing at his eyes.

Luke jumped up and began to run, straight past the stunned Mr. Kerr, toward the town center, screaming at the top of his lungs. He glanced back to see Jumbo, back in the car, careering off down Madison Street, swerving from side to side, nearly smashing into a power pole before correcting and driving around the far corner.

Luke's legs gave out and dumped him back on the ground as blue and red lights swept over him. In confusion, he watched the colors paint the sidewalk around him for a moment; then he looked up to see a Johnson County sheriff's car. An immense weight lifted off his shoulders. It was the county sheriffs' department. They were the serious police. The Iowa City police were really just there to keep order on the campus. But the Johnson County sheriffs were the real deal.

Now they'd have to listen.

Luke managed to stand and moved toward the car, but the officer got out and motioned with a hand for him to stay where he was on the sidewalk.

The officer approached. Luke started to talk, but the officer cut him off. "Are you Luke McKay?" he asked.

Luke nodded, wondering how the officer knew his name. He glanced down the road at Mr. Kerr, who was slowly getting to his feet.

Of all the unlikely rescuers.

"Are you Luke McKay?" the officer repeated, and stated Luke's address.

"Yes," Luke said, looking back and nodding urgently, "and I know where Ms. Sheck is being—"

He cut Luke off again. "Luke McKay, you have been implicated in the looting of the Iowa University Library, and I am hereby taking you into custody as a juvenile suspect."

"I know," Luke said. "But that's not important anymore—"

"Sir, I am going to have to ask you to go ahead and be quiet while I inform you of the rights that you have as a juvenile suspect in a crime," the officer said.

"Listen to me!" Luke cried. "My teacher was kidnapped and—"

"Sir, I am going to ask you *again* to remain silent while I inform you of your rights. If you do not comply with this request, I will be forced to restrain you."

"You're going to cuff me?" Luke shouted. "But—"

"Last chance, kid," he said, pulling the handcuffs from his belt.

24. THE GOOD/BAD COP

His name was Detective Dinning, but he told Luke that he could call him Glenn.

He was the good cop *and* the bad cop.

He'd talk kindly and gently, gaining Luke's trust, and the next second, without warning, he'd slam his fist onto the table and his voice would go from a chatty tone to a shout.

Maybe they can't afford the good cop, Luke thought. Budgets must have been a bit tight at the Johnson County sheriff's office.

Glenn looked at the blurred image on Luke's cell phone and turned it back to him. "And this is Laetitia Sheck, you say?" (Good cop.)

Luke didn't know her name was Laetitia but nodded anyway.

It could have been anyone. It might not even have been a person. The image was so blurred that it was useless. Luke had taken three photos, but they were all the same. Blurred. Unrecognizable.

"It doesn't matter if you believe me or not. How long would it take you to send a car out to the airport and check in the windows of the jet?" Luke asked.

Glenn made a small movement with his head as he shrugged. "Not long. But it's private property, so technically we'd need a search warrant."

Luke sucked in a deep breath. He wanted to scream at this man but knew that would only make matters worse. Why wouldn't he listen to reason?

"Glenn, if you waste time on a search warrant and Mueller takes off in his plane with Ms. Sheck, you might never find her. Send out a car. Just have a quick look. It'll prove that everything I am saying is true."

"You're telling me to send a car?" (Bad cop.) "You don't tell me what to do. You're in a lot of trouble, kid. You do what you're told to do!"

Luke began to feel removed from his body, as if he were watching the scene being played out by actors, instead of being part of it. *Stay calm,* he thought.

"Why are you avoiding my eyes?" Glenn pointed a finger at his own right eye to illustrate his point. "Are you lying to me?"

Luke forced himself to focus on the man's face, but the feeling of detachment remained. His voice said, "If I'm lying, you'll find out real fast."

"You'll never die of a heart attack, will you?" Glenn said.

"What?"

"You're telling me your teacher has been kidnapped, you've been chased by thugs with guns, arrested by the police, and you're as calm as a Hindu cow. You're not even sweating."

Luke watched the drama unfolding in front of him with interest and heard himself ask, "What would sweating accomplish?"

"Might help me believe you, you lying little ratbag." (Bad cop still.)

"But if I'm not lying and you do nothing, you'll look like a real moron." Luke expected an explosion from the bad cop for that remark, but the good cop appeared instead.

Glenn smiled. "Wouldn't be the first time and it won't be the last. But you say that this Mullins, Mueller, whatever, is really after this book. So he won't be in a hurry to leave if he hasn't got it."

"He knows I saw Ms. Sheck," Luke said, "so right now he could do anything."

Glenn put his hands flat on the desk and leaned back in his chair. Luke tensed, wondering which cop he was getting next.

The interview (interrogation?) room was a small paneled office at the rear of the police station in city hall. There was no mirrored window like on TV shows, but two cameras mounted high on the ceiling recorded everything.

Luke's mother was in a brightly lit waiting room by the main entrance, and he couldn't imagine what she was thinking or feeling.

Bad Cop Glenn said, "Come on, kid, admit it. You're making up the whole thing to try and get yourself out of trouble."

"Send a car to the airport," Luke said. *Stop being an idiot!*

"Your fingerprints were found at the library, and one of the news crews caught you on tape climbing over the wall of the ramp. You're up the creek and your paddle ain't working."

"Hangar two." *Just listen instead of talking for once!*

"And all this crap about a rich book collector trying to steal a book that he could simply buy just doesn't make sense. Why not make up something simpler?"

"Because I didn't make it up," Luke said. "Send a car to the airport." *How hard could that be?*

"That's the only thing that's got me wondering." The good cop was back again. "Why would an intelligent kid like you make up a story that's so preposterous that you'd be caught out in a second?"

Luke said nothing.

"Where is this book?" Glenn asked.

"At home," Luke replied. "It's well hidden."

"Tell me where," Glenn said, picking up his pen.

"Send a car to the airport," Luke said, "and I'll show you where."

"I don't negotiate," Bad Cop thundered, slamming his hand down on the table, but the sunshine came out immediately: "But we'll go to your house. If this book really exists, then I'll think about it."

"I'm not moving until you send a car," Luke said. "Mueller

has a nuclear bomb, and you're sitting here doing nothing."

"Ah, yes, the nuclear bomb." Glenn sighed.

He checked some of his notes and said, "You saw the nuclear bomb plans for just a minute or so, yet you were able to reproduce them from memory. That's some amazing memory you have."

"Thank you." Luke ignored the sarcasm.

"With a memory like that, you'd be able to tell me the badge number of the cop who picked you up," Glenn said.

The feeling of dislocation slipped away, and Luke found himself back in his own body—part of the play, no longer sitting in the audience.

"His name was Officer Aaron Fayers," Luke said.

"I didn't ask you his name." Glenn leaned back and folded his arms across his chest. "Again, it seems that someone with a memory like yours would have no trouble with a badge number."

"I hadn't finished," Luke said. "His badge number was 488015. Would you like to know the license plate of his car?"

Glenn nodded, so Luke told him, then said, "When we arrived at the police station, there were six other vehicles in the yard." He listed the license plates of those vehicles, then added the security code Glenn had punched into the lock on the rear door of the station.

Glenn unfolded his arms and stared at him for a moment. Luke struggled with the urge to look at the floor, or the ceiling, or the desk, or his hands.

"Send a car to the airport," Luke said. "What harm can it do?"

Glenn made that funny half shrug again and picked up a telephone off the desk. "Janice, it's Glenn. . . . No, we're in the middle of it now. Tell her I'll see her as soon as I can. Can you do me a favor and ask Matt to swing past the municipal airport? Hangar two. See if there is a private jet in there with call sign . . ."

Luke recited the registration number, and Glenn repeated it into the phone. "If there is, see if he can have a quiet look in one of the windows. Unofficial. Check if there's anyone inside." He looked at Luke and listened for a moment, then said, "I'm not sure, but if so, call me straight-away."

He hung up the phone with a quick thanks and a goodbye.

"The trouble you're in is going to get worse if you've made all that up," he said.

"I just hope you're not too late," Luke replied.

They left through the rear entrance. No handcuffs. No point, really. Glenn knew who Luke was and where he lived. Where could a fifteen-year-old kid run to anyway?

Luke thought of his mother still waiting at the front of the police station and felt bad.

Glenn's car was unmarked, a big Ford wagon that made a throaty noise when he started it. It was only ten or twelve blocks from the police station to his house, and they were there within minutes.

"Don't go running off anywhere," Glenn said, "or I'll hunt

you down." He smiled to let Luke know that he was joking. Maybe.

Luke led him down the side path of the house to the ash dump. "Here," he said, opening the heavy, rusted metal cover and reaching down inside. He brushed away the top layer of ash and felt around for the plastic covering. But he couldn't find it. He dug deeper into the ash. His fingers scraped concrete, and he looked at Glenn in a panic.

"It's not there!" he said.

To give Glenn credit, he actually looked a little disappointed. Luke thought he was really a good cop at heart.

"Anywhere else you want to look?" Glenn asked.

"No, it was here," Luke said in desperation. "Right here. And nobody knew except Tommy, me, and Godzilla!"

"Godzilla?" Glenn sighed. "Tell me all about it back at the station. Or will you have a different story by then?"

"It was here." Luke almost screamed it.

Mueller had it. That was the only thing that made any sense. Someone must have told him where it was.

"He's got Tommy!" Luke said with a sudden horrible certainty.

"Come on," Glenn said, and led the way back up the path to his car.

As Glenn reached the corner of the house, he coughed and his hands shot up in the air. He bent over and began to sag, and Luke couldn't comprehend what was going on until he saw the big man in the black ski mask, the aerosol can, and every fine droplet of spray that was drifting toward his face. Luke tried not to breathe in, but it was already too late. The last thing he saw was Godzilla, the giant squirrel, halfway up the tree outside their house, an acorn clutched in his paws. He was looking at Luke and seemed to be shaking his head disapprovingly, and then everything started to fade.

PART III
THE RIVER

There are three classes of people:
Those who see.
Those who see when they are shown.
Those who do not see.
—Leonardo da Vinci

25. CHILDREN OF THE WOLVES

Luke's grandmother was watching him when he woke. She was seated in a plush leather chair opposite him, and she was holding a gun.

But that made no sense at all.

Luke's grandmother lived in Dunedin, New Zealand. And she didn't own a gun.

There was a constant rushing noise outside his bedroom window, and he turned to look, surprised to see that it was so small, and oval. He glanced back at his grandmother, and it wasn't his grandmother at all. It was someone completely different but someone he knew.

His eyes were blurry and unfocused from having just woken, and he tried to rub them, but his hands would not move. Looking down, he saw they were fastened with a plastic tie.

He blinked a couple of times to clear his eyes and looked at the woman again.

It was the old lady with the groceries from the Central Hotel.

But why did she have a gun?

"Hello, Luke," she said.

How did she know his name?

"Hi, Luke," another voice said, and he turned his head groggily to his left to see his teacher Ms. Sheck.

For a brief moment, he thought he might be in trouble at school again, and then consciousness returned with a crash and a throbbing pain in his temple, and he realized that he really was in trouble. But far bigger trouble than he could ever be in at school.

He was in the jet. Mueller's jet!

The inside of the jet was divided into two sections—individual seats and sofas. He was sitting in a group of four seats, two rows of two, facing each other with a polished wooden table in the center.

Near the front of the plane, a leather sofa ran sideways up to a bulkhead and a door, behind which he guessed was the cockpit.

He looked again at Ms. Sheck. Her hair and clothes were disheveled and sweaty, and she looked like she had been crying, if not today, then earlier. Tommy sat opposite her.

Mueller sat on the sofa with Mumbo, discussing something in a low voice.

Jumbo was nowhere in sight, and Luke wondered if he was flying the plane.

"Who are you?" Luke asked with a thick tongue.

The old lady smiled, but it was without humor. "My name is Gerda Mueller," she said.

The pistol rested on her lap, but her hand was on the grip.

Gerda Mueller. For some reason it had never occurred to Luke that Mueller might be married.

"The police know everything," Luke said. "Whatever you're planning, it's over."

She shook her head and gave the same smile. "It's not over. It hasn't yet started."

He glanced at Ms. Sheck and Tommy, but they both had blank expressions.

"I told them where the book was," Tommy said. "I'm sorry, Luke." He looked as though he was about to burst into tears. "They said they'd hurt me."

Luke didn't blame him. The spy-kid fantasy had just collided with the hard wall of reality, and it wasn't nice.

He'd have done the same, and he told Tommy so.

Mueller had Luke's backpack open on the floor in front of the sofa and was going over the rough sketch of the nuclear bomb that Luke had drawn at the engineering department, comparing it to his own original plans.

"You did this from memory?" he said. "Very impressive."

Impressing Mueller was the least of Luke's concerns.

Ms. Sheck said, "Tommy told me what you boys did. That was very brave."

"I don't understand why they kidnapped you," Luke said.

Ms. Sheck looked bitterly at Mueller, seated at the front of the cabin. "It was the book. *Leonardo's River.* I recognized it immediately," she said. "At least I thought I did. I'd read about it in some library journal. When I got home, I checked it out on the Internet and found Mr. Mueller's email address."

She studied her fingernails, shaking her head. "I emailed him and he called me about five minutes later. I don't even know how he got my number. We talked about it, and he sounded so excited. I was really pleased. I couldn't wait to tell Claudia Smith and the media—everyone. It would be a huge news story. But Mueller asked me not to. Not until he'd positively identified the book. That made sense. It would be embarrassing to make all that fuss only to find out it was the wrong book. Next thing I knew, he was at my door demanding to know what I had done with it. But I hadn't done anything with it."

"No," Luke said. "We had."

"I've been held on this plane for days," Ms. Sheck said. "I've lost track of how many. I tried screaming, but I think it's soundproof."

Luke said, "Are you guys nuts? This is kidnapping. The cops will hunt you down wherever you go. Wherever you take us."

Gerda toyed with the pistol on her lap. "They will look. But it will be a while before they even know where to start, and by then it will be too late."

"What do you mean, too late?" Luke asked with a sudden chill down his spine.

Gerda looked directly into his eyes and said, "They will not find you. You will be gone—"

"Gone where?" Tommy interrupted.

"They will be gone," Gerda continued. "The world as you know it will be gone. In the context of that, what is the importance of a small kidnapping or a short nap for a couple of police officers?"

The world as you know it will be gone.

This had begun with a book, but now it was clear they were involved in something much deeper. Something way over their heads.

That book appeared now, out of Mueller's briefcase. He held it delicately, as if it was valuable treasure rather than just a very old, and very boring, book.

Gerda, too, was staring at the book. It was as if she were unable to take her eyes off it. Clearly it had some kind of power over them. "The last piece of the puzzle," Gerda murmured.

Mueller noticed her gaze, and they shared a smile.

"You're mad," Tommy said. "You and your husband. You're both mad."

Gerda laughed. "You are wrong. On both counts. We are not mad, and Erich is not my husband."

"Yet you share the same last name," Ms. Sheck said.

"Naturally," Gerda said. "He is my brother."

"You're a Werewolf, aren't you?" Luke asked.

"Of course," she said. She seemed proud and sad at once. "One of the very few. The years of hiding and running have taken their toll on our numbers."

"You've lived in hiding for sixty years?" Tommy asked.

"No, not all that time," she said. "But in the early years, just after the war, yes. It was not safe for us to emerge. I was born in the bunkers, and that was the world I knew, for many, many years." She closed her eyes. "The first time I saw blue sky was on my twelfth birthday, and oh, let me tell you, it was the most wondrous birthday present a young girl could wish for."

They remained silent, letting her speak.

"There were many of us then, children of the Wolves.

Entrusted with the great plan. But the others now are gone, from old age or illness. Only my brother and I remain."

She glanced up toward the front of the cabin. "Of course, there are sympathizers. Hired help. But there is no one else who could understand what it was like to have stayed in hiding as the Reich crumbled around us—as invaders from the east and the west looted and ravaged our beautiful cities."

"You started it," Tommy mumbled, but she was lost in her memories.

Luke shifted in his seat, and her grip tightened on the pistol, raising it slightly toward him.

"Because I am old and ramble about the past, do not think that I am sentimental or weak," she said. "I have waited all my life for this moment. I have spent my life running and hiding, enduring things that should not be endured. But when the Reich is restored, I will be a princess. The sons of diplomats and kings will court me with smiles and flowers. I will . . ." She trailed off, closing her eyes again, her head, no doubt, filled with elegant halls and chamber orchestras and dances with handsome young men.

"What 'great plan' did Hitler entrust you with?" Luke asked, but Gerda Mueller was far away, swaying to some inner music.

"She's mad," Ms. Sheck said, but Luke wasn't so sure that she was. Not in the way that Ms. Sheck meant.

In a burst of understanding, it all came together. Who they were. What they were really planning. Luke had finally figured out the secret, hidden for more than a century, of the most boring book in the world.

26. THE LAIR

It was dark when they landed, but the airport was ablaze with lights. The sign over the main terminal announced SALZBURG.

The plane taxied to a private hangar, and they waited on board for ages while Mueller and Mumbo disappeared. Paperwork, Luke guessed, or maybe bribes.

A large black van was inside the hangar when Luke and the others finally emerged from the plane. The lights were off in the hangar, but it was well lit by the glare of the runway lights.

Tommy was right behind Luke as they walked from the plane to the van. He moved as close as he could and whispered, "There's an emergency GPS locator beacon built into my backpack. If I can get to it and activate it, people will come looking for us."

Luke glanced around and saw Tommy's backpack, and his shredded one, in the hands of Jumbo.

There were about twelve seats in the van, but Jumbo made them sit on a single row, in the center, while he and Gerda sat behind them, guns at the ready. Then he put the backpacks on the floor underneath his seat.

Mueller sat up front with Mumbo, who was driving.

Luke forced himself to ignore the guns and the fear and to concentrate on Tommy's backpack as the glow of the airport lights slipped away behind them. The van circled around half of a figure eight–style junction and onto the highway, the autobahn.

There had to be a way to get to the backpack. Obviously he couldn't just go and grab it. If he'd had a bit of string or number eight wire, he might have been able to hook it somehow and try dragging it underneath the seats. But he didn't, and he was pretty sure Gerda and Jumbo would have noticed that. Still, there had to be a way.

The big van traveled fast, switching at one point onto a different autobahn via a big looping off-ramp that took them through farmland.

At a village called Neu-Anif, the van exited the autobahn and turned onto a smaller road that began to twist and wind as they climbed.

More signposts flew past, names Luke did not recognize: St. Leonhard. Schaden. Marktschellenberg. And eventually, one Luke did recognize, one he had been expecting.

Berchtesgaden.

At some point, without customs, immigration, or a barrier of any kind, they had crossed into Germany. Now they were in the alpine resort of Berchtesgaden.

Luke knew the name from the research he had done in the library. It was now a resort and a tourist attraction. But in the 1940s it was the location of the holiday homes for most of the top Nazi leaders, including Adolf Hitler.

It was also the site of the alpine fortress—the National Redoubt—from which Hitler had promised to strike back with secret weapons at one minute past twelve.

Luke had a horrible feeling that the clock was ticking toward midnight.

The van slowed in the mountains and stopped amid a thick forest. Mumbo opened the side door and motioned them out. Luke was confused but looked at Ms. Sheck and saw deep terror in her eyes.

Both Mumbo and Mueller covered them with guns, and the other two followed them out of the van to the side of the road.

"Get it done." Mueller spoke in German, but Tommy translated it for them under his breath. "Make sure the bodies are not found."

Luke glanced desperately around at the others.

Tommy, the kid who could talk his way out of anything, seemed to be in shock, unmoving, a statue, a horrified look frozen on his face.

Ms. Sheck had turned white.

Jumbo limped in front of them, sneering as he stared into Luke's eyes. He raised his pistol, but Gerda moved over and put a hand on his arm.

"Erich," she said, shaking her head slowly.

Mueller looked at her. "What does it matter?" he asked. "In a few days none of this will matter at all."

"That's right," she said. "In a few days none of this will matter at all, so for now, let us not be monsters. They are children. As we once were."

Mueller gazed at her for a while, then shook his head. "Whatever you want," he said. "But make sure they cannot escape."

Luke closed his eyes and clasped his hands together to stop them from shaking. He had a sudden, urgent need to pee.

Let us not be monsters, Gerda had said. But Erich *was* a monster, someone who would kill others without feeling bad about it. And yet, he did not want to show that in front of his little sister.

They were loaded back into the van and driven higher into the mountains. A sign was caught for a moment in the headlights: Obersalzberg.

Here were the bunkers, Luke remembered from the library books, dug deep into the hillsides, beneath the buildings of the town. The last defenses of the Third Reich.

Somewhere near them was the Eagle's Nest—Hitler's mountaintop chalet, with spectacular views of the surrounding alps.

He glanced behind to see Jumbo rummaging through the contents of Tommy's backpack. He examined the night-vision goggles, then put them back and pulled out the lock pick. He looked at Tommy appraisingly, impressed, Luke thought, with Tommy's cool toys.

Luke put his mouth as close as he could to Tommy's ear and whispered, "The GPS—how do you activate it?"

Tommy's voice was a bare murmur in return. "It's built into the backpack. The switch is under the left shoulder strap, at the top. What are you going to do?"

"When we get out," Luke whispered, "Jumbo is going to give me the backpack."

Tommy frowned, not quite believing, then shrugged.

"Stop talking," Gerda said.

The van climbed along steep mountain roads, lined on one side with tall fir and spruce trees, their branches white and bloated with snow. The other side dropped away in a sheer cliff face. Luke began to sway in his seat, letting his head loll about a little.

"What's wrong, Luke?" Ms. Sheck asked with concern.

"I'm not sure," Luke said. "I just feel really dizzy."

"Put your head between your legs for a moment," she said, snapping a look around behind her at Gerda and Jumbo. "Is that all right?"

They said nothing, which Luke took as a yes, and he put his head low between his knees.

Jumbo's big feet were stretched under the seat in front of him, which happened to be Luke's seat. Luke kept his head between his knees and carefully reached down to Jumbo's shoes, untying the laces in tiny, gentle movements, then taking one lace from each shoe and tying them together, leaving plenty of slack.

He waited a few minutes before raising his head and announcing, "I feel better now, thanks."

The road turned to the right, skirting around a small forest and climbing up to a brightly lit building ahead.

Some overgrown foundations appeared briefly in the lights of the van, and from his memory of the book he had studied, he thought they might have been the ruins of the Berghof, Hitler's holiday home. That was confirmed as they neared the building. A sign on the front of the building announced that it was the Hotel zum Türken, which Luke remembered was just up the road from the Berghof.

The van pulled around the side of the hotel and parked in the large parking lot. Besides the guests' cars, it was deserted at this time of the night.

"Out," Mueller barked.

Ms. Sheck opened the van door and stepped down. Luke indicated to Tommy with a nod that he should go in front, so Tommy rose and pushed past Luke's seat.

"You too," Jumbo said menacingly.

Luke got out of the van. He took a couple of steps, then turned back just in time to see Jumbo step down—or try to.

Luke had tied Jumbo's laces loosely enough to allow him to shuffle within the confines of the van without noticing that his laces were tied together, but the moment he tried to step down to the ground, the laces snagged, and he tripped and went flying, landing facedown on the asphalt.

Tommy's backpack flew out of Jumbo's arms, landing by Luke's feet. Luke picked it up. He quickly activated the beacon as Jumbo stood, wiping blood from his nose and trying to work out what had happened. He looked at Luke with daggers in his eyes, clearly convinced that Luke was somehow responsible.

"Are you okay?" Luke asked innocently.

Jumbo scowled as Luke meekly handed him the backpack.

Gerda stepped down, carrying Luke's backpack, and the whole group entered the hotel through a rear entrance.

There was nobody around, and Mueller led them to a door, which he unlocked. Behind it was a flight of stairs leading into a cellar. It was musty and looked unused. A rack of shelving lined one wall. Mueller reached up, flicking a hidden catch, and slid the shelving aside.

It revealed a strong metal door, which he unlocked as well, this time with a large, old-fashioned key.

The door led to a brick-lined tunnel and a circular flight of stairs that took them deep underground.

Luke sighed. All that trouble to set off the beacon and now they were descending into the earth, where the signal would be lost.

More tunnels led off in other directions as they reached a lower passageway, and doors were set into the sides of the main corridor.

It was an underground bunker.

The lair of the Werewolves.

27. THE DISCOVERY

"Do either of you have any idea what this is all about?" Ms. Sheck asked.

They were sitting on the hard concrete floor of a bunker cell, solid rusted metal bars preventing any thought of escape.

Tommy shook his head.

"I think I do. Bits of it anyway," Luke said.

Jumbo's bull-shaped head and thick neck appeared at the gate as he checked on them. Luke waited quietly for him to leave, looking around at the dank, dreary walls of the bunker.

So this was where Gerda had spent her childhood. Deep underground in a world made of concrete and brick, lit only by murky yellow electric globes, learning to hate the world that had trapped her here. Dreaming of a time when Nazi Germany would rise again and she would emerge into the sunshine, as one of the chosen ones. The golden children of the Third Reich.

Jumbo's footsteps faded away down the corridor.

"I think Leonardo da Vinci made a really big discovery," Luke said. "Something so incredibly powerful that he knew he needed to keep it supersecret."

"Some new kind of weapon?" Tommy asked, but Luke shook his head.

"No, not a weapon. A . . ." He hesitated, trying to decide the right word. "A machine. I'll get to that. I think Benfer somehow found out about Leonardo's discovery. He must have found Leonardo's drawings."

"How is that possible?" Ms. Sheck asked.

"Beats me. Benfer grew up in Italy. Maybe he stumbled across another of Leonardo's hidden laboratories," Luke said.

"So what did he do with them?" Tommy raised an eyebrow.

"I think that when he realized what he had found, he knew, just like Leonardo, that this discovery would be really, really bad if it got out. It could never be made public. So he hid the drawings somewhere they would never be found. I think the book is some sort of treasure map. It tells you where to find Leonardo's drawings."

"Where?" Ms. Sheck asked.

"I have no idea," Luke said. "I haven't finished the book." He shut his eyes for a moment. "There's one clue that I think is important, but I haven't been able to figure it out yet. A character in Benfer's book: Johann Heidenberg. Benfer must have put him in the book for a reason. I was going to Google him or do some more research in the library, but we ended up here instead."

"Did you say Johann Heidenberg?" Ms. Sheck asked.

"Yes," Luke said, and spelled the name out.

A strange look came over her face. "I know that name," she said. "He was a real person. We studied him in lit history at college. I remember him clearly; it was funny, because of his last name."

"Funny ha-ha, or funny peculiar?" Tommy asked.

Ms. Sheck didn't seem to hear him. "He lived in the late fifteenth century," she said.

"Around the same time as Leonardo," Luke said.

"Yes, probably," Ms. Sheck said. "He changed his name to something else later, but I could only remember his original name, because of what he did."

"What did he do?" Luke asked.

"He was German. He was an abbot who studied the occult—"

"Was Benfer into black magic?" Tommy interrupted, wide-eyed.

"Shut up and listen," Luke said.

Ms. Sheck continued. "Heidenberg is most famous for a book called *Steganographia*, which is supposed to be about magic and dark spirits, but in reality it's about secret codes and messages. All the secret code stuff is hidden inside the words of the book."

"Are you sure about this?" Luke asked.

"Yes. *Steganography* means the art of hiding something in plain sight. Hiding information inside a message or a book. That's why I always remembered his name. Johann Heidenberg. We called him Johann Hide-in-Book."

"So that's it," Luke said. "That's where Benfer hid the

drawings. In the book! He must have destroyed Leonardo's original plans but secretly put the information in *Leonardo's River*."

A door slammed somewhere in the depths of the bunker, a harsh metallic clang that reverberated off the hard rock walls of their prison. Luke jumped a little. The noise brought with it a cool fist of air. One of the lamps in the corridor flickered and dimmed for a moment with a sharp buzzing sound.

"Why?" Ms. Sheck asked. "Why keep the information at all if it was so dangerous?"

"I guess he couldn't bring himself to destroy it," Luke said. "I mean, this was the most amazing discovery in the history of science. Maybe he couldn't bear to see it lost forever. But he made sure that the book was so boring, so mind-numbingly tedious, that nobody would ever read it."

"Somehow the Nazis must have found out about Leonardo's discovery," Tommy said.

Ms. Sheck said, "The Nazis stole thousands of pieces of artwork, from many famous painters, including several of Leonardo's pieces. They must have found their own copy of Leonardo's drawings. Perhaps an incomplete copy, or an earlier copy."

"Like a first draft," Tommy said.

"Yeah." Luke nodded. "They still needed Benfer's book. That's what Gerda said about 'the last piece of the puzzle.' They must have traced the other drawings somehow to Benfer and realized the truth about his book. But they were stuck. They couldn't find the book, so they couldn't complete their 'great plan.'"

"Until now," Ms. Sheck said.

"Until now," Luke agreed.

"I still don't get it," Tommy said. "What was this fantastic discovery, this 'machine,' if it wasn't some kind of super-weapon?"

Luke looked at them both, wondering if they would think he was nuts. Since he'd figured it out, even *he* thought he was going nuts. But it was the only thing that made sense, the only thing that connected all the dots.

"In the book there was this quotation," Luke said. "I was just starting to read it when I fell asleep, and it didn't really register at the time."

"From Leonardo?" Tommy asked.

"Yeah," Luke said. "He said, 'In rivers, the water that you touch is the last of what has passed and the first of that which comes; so with present time.'"

Tommy nodded. "I remember that one from the book I read in the library."

"But that's not the whole quotation," Luke said. "Benfer had the rest of it: 'Were it possible to bend time upon itself, as a river twists and turns, then might not we journey across time as we now journey across a river?'"

Tommy looked confused, and Ms. Sheck looked horrified.

Luke said, "When Hitler talked about striking back at *one minute past twelve,* everyone thought he meant *at the very last minute.* But what I think he really meant was *from another time!*"

"Another time?" Ms. Sheck was incredulous.

"It's something to do with the rare-earth magnets," Luke

said. "Some way of bending time. The drawings of the *Vitruvian Man* are a blueprint. A diagram of how to do it."

"That nude dude in a circle is a blueprint?" Tommy said skeptically.

"It's not just a circle," Luke said. "There is a whole series of drawings, remember. When you put them all together, it's a nude dude in a cube. And a sphere."

"A diagram of a time machine," Ms. Sheck said.

"But why does . . ." Tommy trailed off as he caught on to what Ms. Sheck and Luke had already realized.

Mueller didn't have an atomic bomb. He didn't need one. All he needed were the plans.

Mueller was not planning to destroy the world.

He was going to change the course of history.

"Oh, crap," Luke said. "Do you remember when Mueller and Gerda said 'in a few days none of this will matter at all'? I couldn't understand what they could do in just a few days. There's only one explanation. It wasn't a copy of Leonardo's drawings that the Nazis discovered; they must have found his time machine itself."

"In Italy?" Tommy asked.

"I guess. They probably packed it up and shipped it here to the bunkers, piece by piece."

"You mean they've already got the time machine?" Tommy's eyes were saucers.

"I think so," Luke breathed. "But they didn't know how to use it. It wasn't a set of plans they needed. It was an instruction manual."

"And now they've got one," Ms. Sheck said.

28. PRINCESS

"You know how Leonardo invented all those crazy things, like submarines and helicopters and hang gliders?" Tommy said, and Luke looked over at him, guessing what he was going to say next. "I've just been thinking that maybe he didn't invent them at all. Maybe he saw them."

"You mean he traveled to the future?" Ms. Sheck said.

"Yeah."

Luke nodded; he'd been thinking exactly the same thing. "He saw some of these things and went back and tried to design them, but using fifteenth-century technology."

There were murmuring voices and footsteps in the corridor outside their cell. Luke glanced up to see Mueller and Mumbo walk past the barred gate.

Each of them wore the black uniform of a 1940s German SS officer.

"They're getting ready to leave," Luke said.

On a trip like no other, he thought. *A journey back to World War II.*

"We've got to stop them," Ms. Sheck said.

"How?" Luke asked, looking at the thick bars of the gate.

"I don't know how, but we have to. The Nazis came very close to inventing an atomic bomb in the 1940s," Ms. Sheck said. "With Mueller's plans, they will succeed, and they will win the war."

"We'll be Nazis," Tommy said glumly.

"I don't think so," Luke said. "I don't think we'll exist."

Tommy looked up sharply.

"Well," Luke said, "if you change history that much, you'll change everything. Your grandparents might never meet. Your parents won't be born. So you will never be born. Same for everyone else we know. It'll be a completely different world, with different people in it."

Luke examined the gate again. Surely there had to be some way to get out. But it looked solid, if brown and rusted, and it still looked just as locked. It was secured with a heavy-duty modern brass padlock.

Maybe with Tommy's lock pick they might have had a chance, but that was in his backpack. And the Werewolves had that.

"If we could get out of here," Luke asked Ms. Sheck, "what would we do?"

"I don't know," she said. "But if they get back to the 1940s with those plans, then that's the end of everything."

As Luke was standing at the door, Jumbo limped past, also in the uniform of the SS. He scowled at them.

Luke scowled back. Mean faces weren't going to scare him. Hitler with a nuclear bomb . . . *that* scared him.

He tried to shake the bars but they didn't move. He scanned around the tiny cell for anything that they could use to lever them apart, but there was nothing.

When Luke turned back toward the front of the cell, Gerda was there, watching him, the pistol in her hand.

"What are you going to do?" Luke asked in an unsteady voice.

She glanced down absently at the pistol. "Oh, don't be afraid," she said. "I'm not going to hurt you. Erich and the boys are getting ready to go, and he wants me to keep an eye on you to make sure that you stay exactly where you are."

They weren't going anywhere, Luke thought, but he said nothing.

After a while, Mueller appeared with a wooden chair and placed it for her a few feet back from the cell.

"Thank you, Erich," Gerda said, taking the seat and resting the pistol on her knee.

"We are about to depart," Mueller said. "I will see you in the New World."

A glow seemed to come over Gerda and her eyes glazed. Luke sensed her mind was elsewhere—daydreaming about a different life, perhaps. One of glittering riches and fancy parties with handsome young men. "*Auf wiedersehen*, Erich," she said, almost in a trance.

"Heil Hitler!" He snapped out a Nazi salute.

She returned it with a tired lift of her arm and then stood. They embraced for a short moment.

Mueller turned, his heels clicking together, and marched back down the corridor.

Heading for the past. For his new future.

Luke watched him go.

"Gerda," he said softly after a while, and she looked up. "Are you really going to let him do this?"

"We have been planning this all of our lives," she said. "Since decades before you were born. We have waited a long time for this moment."

She looked down, and the pain and the strain of those years of hiding, living underground, showed clearly on her face.

Ms. Sheck stood and moved beside Luke. She said, "You know what will happen if Hitler gets the atomic bomb, don't you?"

Gerda said nothing.

"Millions will die," Ms. Sheck said. "Hitler will use the bomb indiscriminately. On London, maybe. Or Washington. Moscow probably, the first one. The United States will retaliate with its own atomic bombs. Berlin, Frankfurt, Munich will cease to exist."

Gerda said nothing, but somehow she looked older and frailer than before.

"Hitler will use the bombs without mercy," Ms. Sheck said. "He murdered millions of innocent Jews in the concentration camps and—"

"That's a lie," Gerda snapped, her eyes burning at Ms. Sheck. "That is propaganda made up by the Allies after the war to try and make us out to be evil monsters."

"It is no lie," Ms. Sheck said. "There are thousands of

photos of those camps, and evidence of what went on there."

"All created by the Allies," Gerda said.

"All of it true," Ms. Sheck said. "I wish it wasn't. My grandfather survived one of those camps. His mother and father, his brothers and sisters did not."

Gerda looked away, no longer wanting to meet Ms. Sheck's eyes.

"I will be a princess," she whispered, her eyes faraway.

"You are condemning me to death," Luke said. "Me and Tommy and billions of other kids all over the world."

"You will never have existed," Gerda said. "That's not the same as being killed."

"It is from where I stand," Luke said.

"I will be a princess," she said again, and rose a little unsteadily.

"In a nuclear wasteland!" Luke shouted in frustration as she tottered away down the long corridor.

He left the gate and sank back down against the wall of the cell, close to despair. He had the feeling that at any moment he would just vanish. Dissolve into nothing, as Mueller and his cohorts changed the past. Changed *his* past.

If by some miracle he did still exist, if his grandparents did still meet, and his father still met his mother, would he be the same person he was now?

Most likely I would be a Nazi, Luke thought. *Everyone would be Nazis.* He stood, walking around the cell one more time.

Tommy stared at the floor. Ms. Sheck smiled at him, but there was no trace of hope in it.

He looked at the bars again. Back on the farm, his dad had often told him there was no problem in the world that couldn't be solved with a little hard work and common sense. But then, his dad had never been stuck in a Nazi prison cell waiting for the world to end.

He forced himself to focus. The cell's left and back walls were rock, as were the floor and ceiling. Given the right tools and enough time, they might have been able to tunnel out, but they had neither tools nor time. The right wall was made of solid concrete blocks.

If he could take the pins out of the hinges, he could open the door that way. But the hinges were welded over top and bottom to prevent exactly that.

All the bars were rusty, though, and the hinges had creaked when they had been forced into the cell. Rusty metal meant weakened metal, but nothing looked weak enough to help them.

He moved along the bars, shaking each one in turn, hoping for one that was loose, but they all held firm.

Okay. What was the weakest point? The bars connected to a long horizontal metal crosspiece at the top and another at the bottom. Two more such crosspieces ran through the middle of the bars, preventing any chance of bending them.

There was no room above or below the bars to squeeze through. Nor on the sides. He rattled the door in its frame and was rewarded by nothing more than a few flakes of rust falling.

Luke moved over to his right, examining the concrete blocks at the end of the wall. One of them didn't look as straight as the others. He pushed on it, but it didn't move. He grasped it by the end, putting his hands through the bars of the cell to do so, and yanked it toward him with all of his strength.

To his surprise, it moved, not even an inch, but it moved. It was loose.

He looked over at the others. "Give me a hand," he said.

"What?" Tommy jumped up, filled with renewed hope that Luke thought was somewhat premature.

"Push on the other end of this block," Luke said. "As hard as you can."

Tommy flattened his hands on the block and shoved. Luke pulled again on the other end, and with a grinding noise, the block shifted. Crumbling sixty-year-old mortar fell out of the gaps between the blocks.

"Again," Luke said.

They shoved again and the block moved more. Gradually, by pulling and shoving, they were able to maneuver the block out of position and slide it forward until it dropped to the ground outside the cell, leaving a small hole in the wall.

Luke froze. "Do you think they heard that?"

There were no sounds from the corridors, and after a moment he turned his attention back to the wall.

The block above the hole was now being held by just a thin strip of mortar.

Luke climbed up on the bars of the cell until he could touch the ceiling and kicked at the block. Two or three good kicks and it fell down onto the block below it, disappearing behind the wall.

Tommy joined in, and they both kicked at the lower block. It, too, shifted, then fell, leaving a human-sized gap in the wall.

Tommy was the first to squeeze through, but Luke was close behind him, with Ms. Sheck right on his heels.

"What do we do now?" Tommy asked as they ran along the corridor in the direction Mueller had taken.

"We have to stop him," Ms. Sheck said, but didn't offer any suggestions how.

Soft music began to wash faintly at Luke's ears. A woman's voice humming, a childlike tune, perhaps a lullaby, familiar even though he had never heard it before. It grew louder and clearer as they neared the end of the corridor, and he recognized the voice. It was Gerda Mueller.

They turned the corner into the next corridor and stopped.

Gerda stood in front of them. Her head was tilted back, her eyes shut. She was lost in some other world, swaying from side to side.

It might have been some small noise they made or a change in the air of the corridor, but she seemed to sense their presence and her eyes sprang open. Her right hand, which had dangled by her side, now came up in their direction. In it was the pistol. Her eyes focused on them, although she continued to hum, as though she didn't realize she was doing it.

Luke took a step forward and readied himself to spring. There was no other option. They couldn't go back. Could he cover the distance in time? If he could weave a bit, throw off her aim, hopefully dodge the first shot and get to her before she could fire a second time . . . If not, then could he, would he, have the courage to throw himself on the gun and give the others time to get to her?

Luke tensed, then relaxed as a warm hand touched him on the shoulder.

"No, Luke," Ms. Sheck said.

She took a step toward Gerda, who instinctively retreated, but the gun did not waver.

Then, to Luke's surprise, Ms. Sheck began to sing. She joined in with Gerda's tune, adding lyrics to the hummed melody.

The words were in a language Luke didn't understand, an ancient language, perhaps. But Ms. Sheck's voice was low and soothing, filling the corridor, enveloping them in a warm musical blanket. Ms. Sheck advanced, one tentative footstep after another, her voice giving color to the dull rock walls of the tunnels.

Luke waited for the shot, for the shudder as the bullet entered Ms. Sheck's delicate frame, for the sudden rush of blood and the last choking gasps of his teacher's life.

Ms. Sheck took another step. Gerda raised the gun slightly higher. *Aiming for the head,* Luke thought.

Only a yard or two away and still there was no shot. It was either the bravest or the stupidest thing Luke had ever seen in his life, or maybe Ms. Sheck had realized, like Luke, that if she didn't do this, then the world as they knew it would be gone forever.

Luke readied himself again to spring. When the gun fired, he would have only seconds to try to get to it before Gerda could fire a second time. Whatever happened to Ms. Sheck with that first shot, he had to ignore it, to ignore her, and focus only on getting to the gun.

A single foot separated the two women, and Luke knew it was now or never. If Gerda was going to pull the trigger, it would have to be before Ms. Sheck got within range to grab the gun.

He raised himself onto the balls of his feet.

But Ms. Sheck did not grab for the pistol, and the pistol did not fire. Ms. Sheck simply moved past the outstretched gun and reached for Gerda.

Gerda stood there trembling as Ms. Sheck put her arms around her and drew her close, one hand pulling Gerda's head down onto her shoulder, as she might comfort a baby.

Next to Luke, Tommy breathed out.

Slowly, the gun lowered, and after a few moments, Luke took it from Gerda's hand before it could slip to the ground. The song trailed off.

Gerda was sobbing. Not huge, chest-wracking sobs, but rather a quiet, tired whimper. Still Ms. Sheck held her, and then abruptly Gerda broke away.

Luke stood next to Ms. Sheck, holding the gun, and Tommy moved up beside them. Together they watched Gerda Mueller, locked in an embrace with an imaginary suitor, her head tilted nobly back, her hips swaying to music that was only in her head, waltzing away down the concrete tunnel of the bunker as if she were dancing through the great halls of Europe.

They said nothing as they watched seventy years of golden dreams turn to dust and slip through her fingers.

29. THE CHAMBER

The long corridors were lit only by overhead bulkhead lights that cast a dim malevolence over them as they hurried through the bunker.

At one point, they came to a dead end and backtracked to a side tunnel with a brick archway. It was narrower than the others, and more and more Luke felt the walls pressing in around him. He could visualize the tons of earth that were above his head, held up by only the concrete roof.

The tunnel seemed to narrow as they went. Their footsteps echoed off the walls, and Luke was certain that Mueller would hear them coming, but there was nothing he could do about it.

Luke had the lead, followed by Ms. Sheck, with Tommy at the rear. They came to another dead end and doubled back. There were many passages leading off the main tunnel, with arrows and words in German handwritten on the walls in faded and chipped white paint.

He couldn't read the signs but was confident that Tommy would say something if any of the signs said "To the Time Machine."

They glanced in a few of the rooms as they passed them. One was obviously set up as Mueller's office, with a computer and a laser printer.

Luke stopped abruptly alongside a small metal door, oval in shape, like a pressure door on a submarine. They had passed it a few minutes ago, and he'd thought nothing of it. But this time something about it seemed odd.

"There are no markings on this door," he said. "All the other doors and tunnels have signs saying where they lead. But this one doesn't."

A long metal pole made a handle in the center of the door. He grabbed it and tried to lift it, but it was too heavy.

Ms. Sheck and Tommy lent their weight, and the handle lifted, one inch, then another, and the door gasped and shuddered open a fraction.

Luke put his shoulder to it and forced it back against the wall.

Behind it, a staircase led down into gathering darkness. It was lit with the same bulkhead lights as the passageways.

The walls here were not the same gray concrete and brick of the tunnels but were cut out of the rock itself.

They were heading deep into the heart of the mountain.

A handrail ran down the left side of the massive staircase, bolted onto the rock wall, and Luke kept a hand on it for safety as he jumped down two or three steps at a time. In places moisture seeped through the rock ceiling, staining the concrete steps below a dirty greenish color.

Luke was out of breath by the time they reached the bottom, despite the fact that they were running downhill.

Another oval door at the foot of the staircase opened into a massive, cavelike hollow. He wasn't sure whether it was a natural cavern in the rock or whether the Nazis had dug it out by hand. Then his attention was drawn to the huge structure in front of them: a wall of gray metal, blanketed with rust.

"Do you have anything metal on you?" Tommy asked.

Luke held up the pistol. "Why?"

"I think it has a magnetic shield," Tommy said. "I wondered if we'd find something like this. A wall of iron that shields the magnets inside."

Luke put down the gun and checked his pockets. They had taken his cell phone away. He still had his watch on, so he put it on the ground by the stairs behind him. He saw Ms. Sheck do the same.

"What are we going to do when we get in there?" she asked.

By now he had a semi-formed plan in his mind, with no real idea if it would work.

"You two distract them, attack them. Do whatever it takes. Buy me some time," Luke said. "Leonardo was very precise about the position of the magnets. Benfer put it all in the book. I'm pretty sure that by adjusting the position, you change the 'bend' in the river of time. While you guys keep them busy, I'm going to try and adjust the magnets. Throw it off a little. Just a few years will do—after the war is finished."

"Send 'em back to the time of the dinosaurs," Tommy said grimly.

"Do whatever you can," Ms. Sheck said.

A narrow opening was cut into the wall, on a diagonal. They slid through, one by one, into the cave.

Immediately, Luke could hear voices, speaking in German, although he could not see Mueller or the others.

Inside the cave, the fine hairs on his arms and legs lifted, and even his scalp felt strange, as though his head were underwater. His ears thrummed.

Ms. Sheck and Tommy came up close on either side of him and they all stared.

The metal wall behind them extended up and over the ceiling of the cave and around each side. In front of them was a huge structure, built from a charcoal-colored substance. It was as big as a house and made of a strange combination of curves and angles, as if someone had taken a giant cube and a giant sphere and melded them together.

Beside him Tommy breathed, "The *Vitruvian Man*."

Leonardo's drawings had been of a sphere and a cube. That sphere and cube now lay in front of them, constructed in intricate detail from rare-earth magnets. This was his chamber. His time machine.

A wooden framework surrounded the chamber. Wooden struts reached down to each odd angle and surface. The struts were calibrated with finely detailed markings, and each had a rope and wedge system for making adjustments.

"This is it," Luke said. "I guess if we mess with those adjustable struts, they could end up anywhere."

On a small table next to the chamber sat a book, and he didn't need to see the cover to know that it was *Leonardo's River.* The blueprint and the user manual for the chamber.

Luke started toward the structure, and at that moment Mueller strode around the corner of the chamber in his menacing black SS uniform.

Luke flattened himself behind another corner of the chamber.

Mueller stooped and ducked under a low rectangular opening in the side of the structure.

He was too late!

Luke launched himself at the rope and wooden strut nearest him. He dug into the rope with his fingernails, hoping to upset the calibration and send them to the wrong place or time. But it was tightly knotted, and before he could make any headway at all, he saw Jumbo and Mumbo dip through the same opening as Mueller.

Into the chamber.

Into the past.

30. NO TIME

Luke dropped the ropes instantly.

"We gotta follow them," he said, peering into the hole that was the entrance to the chamber. His ears fizzed, being so close to the device, but he could see nothing inside but blackness.

"No, we should go and get help," Ms. Sheck said.

"Go where?" Luke asked. "We're deep underground in a bunker system somewhere in the mountains of Bavaria. Even if we found our way out and got to the authorities—and if they believed us—then it would still take days for them to organize some kind of action, and even then what would they do? What could they do? There's no time. We have to go now!"

"Then I will go," she said. "You boys go for help."

"No," Luke said. "No, we should all go."

"You're too young," Ms. Sheck said. "I can't let you do this."

"That doesn't make any sense," Tommy said, picking at

his fingernails. "I'm the only one who can speak German. You wouldn't last a minute in 1940s Germany. It has to be me who goes."

Ms. Sheck opened her mouth, then shut it again. There was no arguing with that.

"I'm coming with you," Luke said.

"But you don't speak German!"

"I'll pretend to be mute, or Polish or something," Luke said. "You can't go chasing after Mueller alone."

"You could pretend to be a moron." Tommy attempted a grin. "You're good at that."

Luke smiled. "Whatever, bro."

Ms. Sheck gave them each a hug. Most of the other guys at school would have been jealous, Luke thought, but somehow it didn't seem like such a big deal after all they'd been through together.

Luke led the way toward the small opening, his hair frizzing up on end; even his nostrils flared with the intensity of the rare-earth magnets that surrounded them.

"Stop!" a voice commanded, and he looked back to see Gerda Mueller advancing into the cave. "Stop!" she said again.

She had been crying. Her eyes were red and puffy, and the paths of tears stained the powder on her cheeks.

"You can't stop us," Luke said. "We have to do this."

Gerda shook her head. "Nazi Germany, in 1944, is at war. You will not last a day without proper papers. And Berchtesgaden at the end of the war was a secure zone. Even the German public was not allowed to enter."

"Then help us," Ms. Sheck said.

Gerda looked away. "Now you are asking too much."

"Are we?" Luke asked. "Is it too much to ask that we stop Adolf Hitler from killing millions of innocent people?"

"Hitler was a great man," Gerda said.

"Hitler was a madman," Tommy said.

"He could have been a great man," Gerda said. "He should have been a great man."

"If you don't help us, Gerda, millions of people will die," Ms. Sheck said. "This time it's not up to Hitler. It's not up to your brother, Erich. Right now, it's on your shoulders. Could you really go dancing and partying knowing that you could have saved so many lives but did nothing?"

There was a long silence.

"Forget about her; forget about the papers," Luke said. "We have to go now or we will lose them."

A small, tired voice seemed to come from somewhere deep inside Gerda. "Wait. We have a few minutes. I know where he is heading. And I can make you the right papers."

She turned and indicated with a glance that they should follow her.

"Thank you, Gerda," Ms. Sheck said.

On the way up the staircase, Gerda said, "From Obersalzberg, Erich will commandeer a car and drive down to Berchtesgaden town, to the Bahnhof, the railway station. In those days, the train to Munich ran just twice a day, so he will wait there for the train. At Munich, he will change trains for Berlin. He is taking the plans directly to the Führer."

"Why 1944?" Luke asked. "Why not take the plans back

to 1939 and give them to Hitler at the start of the war?"

"We did not find the Vitruvian chamber until 1944," she said. "If Erich was to appear, out of nowhere, talking about a project that was yet to exist, he would likely end up in a Gestapo interrogation cell instead of the Führer's private office."

She held on tightly to the handrail as she walked, the stairs difficult for her. She continued. "The settings on the chamber are not so exact either. An inch could throw out your destination by years. Our accuracy is within a month at the best. Erich is aiming for September of 1944, which will still give our scientists time to build the bomb before the end of the war."

At the top of the stairs, she led them down a passageway to the office they had noticed earlier.

From a folder in a drawer in the desk, she took blank identity cards emblazoned with the wolf's hook. In another drawer were official-looking rubber stamps and an ink pad. A laser printer sat on the desk next to the computer, and a digital camera in the corner was connected to a photo printer on a table by the wall. Some old-style paper sat in a tray on the table.

"I'm not good with computers," Gerda said. "But if one of you boys can help, I will tell you what information you will need."

"You bet," Tommy said, settling down behind the computer. He took a quick snap of Luke with the digital camera, and Luke left them to it. He went scouting around through the other offices to see if there was anything they could use.

He found his and Tommy's backpacks and brought them back to the office. There was nothing he wanted from his own, but Tommy's held all sorts of interesting devices.

While Tommy and Gerda finished their IDs, Luke started skimming through *Leonardo's River*. Not bothering to read the text, just flipping through the diagrams and the measurements.

Tommy handed Luke an ID card. It looked odd. It was in German, for sure, but all the writing was backward, mirrored like the plans for the atomic bomb.

There were also some ID papers and a travel permit, mirrored as well.

Luke queried Tommy, but Tommy just shook his head.

"Gerda says that is how they are supposed to be." He shrugged. "Beats me."

Luke looked at it. He was now officially a Werewolf.

Luke handed Tommy his backpack, and his friend's eyes lit up. He dropped to one knee and began sorting through his bag of tricks.

"Nothing metal," Luke reminded him. "Or even with metal in it. It could be disastrous."

"I know," he said. "But a lot of these things are made from aluminum, plastic, and glass. They're spy gadgets, so they're designed to get past metal detectors."

"What about zippers?" Luke asked, glancing quickly at Ms. Sheck. He did not want to take his jeans off in front of her.

"They don't set off metal detectors either," Tommy said.

"But you can't wear jeans in 1940s Germany, or T-shirts. You'll stand out a mile," Ms. Sheck said.

"In 1944 this was my nursery," Gerda said, looking around at the walls. Her eyes seemed to fill with distant memories. "Erich's room was next door. He was about your size. You should find what you need."

She spent a few minutes explaining how they should dress, then handed Luke an aluminum key, shiny and light, and said, "You will need reichsmarks. There is a safe in an office on the other side of the corridor." She walked to the doorway and pointed it out to Luke. "You will find whatever you need in there."

"Why don't you come with us?" Luke asked. "Try and persuade your brother to change his mind."

Her eyes dropped to the floor. "Now you really are asking too much," she said quietly, and Luke realized that in at least part of her heart, she still hoped that her brother would succeed.

They descended again to the chamber, but before they could enter, she reached out and took Tommy's and Luke's hands in hers.

"You are good boys," she said. "Be very careful. My brother is dedicated to this mission and will do anything to see it through."

"You be careful," Ms. Sheck agreed.

"Ms. Sheck," Luke said, "you have to stay right here. Make sure no one goes anywhere near the chamber. If someone adjusts any of these ropes, changes the settings, then we'll have no way to get back."

"I'm not going anywhere," she said. "I'll be waiting right here for you."

Without another word, Luke ducked under the low hatch, and with every fiber of his body now buzzing from the massive magnetic fields that surrounded him, he climbed in toward the center of the chamber.

The buzzing intensified and every hair on his body stood on end. His skin began to crawl as though a million tiny ants were covering him. The muscles in his body began to twitch with a mild electrical shock. His heart seemed to pause its beating.

Then the charcoal-black walls of the chamber were gone. And there was nothing beneath his feet.

He was falling.

31. FORTY-FOUR

Luke's legs buckled underneath him as he landed, more from the shock than the height, which was probably no more than half a yard.

It was pitch-black. He sat still for a moment, stunned, then realized that he had better move before Tommy landed on top of him. He rolled out of the way just as there was a heavy thump and Tommy said, "Ow!"

"You all right?" Luke asked.

"Yeah, I'm good. Where are we?" Tommy asked.

"I think we're exactly where we were," Luke said.

"Then what happened to the chamber?" Tommy asked.

"I don't think they've built it yet," Luke replied.

There was a cracking sound from Tommy's direction, and the cave suddenly filled with a vague green glow.

Tommy had a glow stick in his hand.

It was just enough for them to see that the cave was deserted, although tidy piles of timber and coils of rope were spread around the circumference.

"It looks like they're about to start building it," Tommy said.

Behind them, work had already started on the massive metal wall that would become the shield for the magnetic chamber, and a number of heavy metal plates were stacked near the wall, alongside a cranelike machine, a block and tackle suspended from a tall wooden frame.

Wooden crates full of bolts and nuts sat next to welding equipment.

There was no sign of the components of the chamber itself. That made sense, Luke thought. They couldn't start building the chamber until the shield was completed.

A large white cross had been chalked on the floor, slightly smudged from their landing on top of it.

"*X* marks the spot," Tommy said. "What's that about?"

"That's to help them find their way home," Luke said.

"How's that?" Tommy asked.

"They'd need to return to exactly the same spot to go back through the chamber," Luke said. "So would we. Make sure you don't smudge it any more."

"You bet," Tommy said, stepping quickly away from it.

"I wonder what the date is," Luke said.

It was Monday, November 27, 1944, according to the calendar they found in one of the offices.

"Look at this," Tommy said, holding up his ID papers. In normal time, the words on the paper had been reversed, but now they looked normal.

"How could that be?" Luke asked.

"I think that when you go through the Vitruvian chamber and switch into a different time, everything somehow gets reversed. Like reversing the poles of a magnet."

"Even us?"

"I guess."

Luke pulled up the leg of his jeans and looked at his right knee. He had gashed it pretty badly that night on the bridge. But there was no mark at all. He lifted the left side. There it was. A half-healed wound. It had switched sides!

"Maybe that's why Leonardo wrote lots of his notes backward," Luke realized. "He was actually writing them normally."

"Yeah, but when he brought them back through the chamber, they got mirrored!" Tommy added. "That would also explain why the atomic bomb plans were mirrored when we saw them."

The early hour of the morning was a stroke of luck, as the corridors of the bunker system were deserted. Luke's and Tommy's footsteps echoed eerily. Soft breathing sounds came from the rooms on either side.

They spoke little, for fear of waking someone, and found their way to the room that Gerda said had been Erich's. A metal-framed bunk was in the far corner of the room, and slight stirrings came from the thin shape under the bedclothes.

Tommy remained outside while Luke tiptoed to a small freestanding wooden closet by the bed and searched for the specific clothes that Gerda had suggested. The breathing sounds from the bed stopped abruptly as he shut the closet door, but resumed again after a moment, and he crept out of the room.

A door at the end of the corridor was marked with a large red cross, and on impulse, Luke looked inside, finding a nursing station.

He had an idea. He rummaged through some drawers until he found a long length of bandage, which he wound around his scalp and jaw and fastened with a pin.

He was the victim of an air raid and couldn't speak, he told Tommy. If they needed any more details, Tommy would have to make them up on the spot.

It seemed creepy to Luke to be wearing young Erich Mueller's clothes. But it was even creepier when they finished dressing, in an empty room, and looked at each other. Luke shuddered, looking at Tommy, and knew that Tommy must have felt the same way about him.

They were both dressed in brown shirts, black shorts, and white knee-high socks. The uniform of the *Hitlerjugend*. The Hitler Youth.

The shoes were black leather. They fit Luke okay but were too big for Tommy. He solved that with an extra pair of socks crammed into the toes.

There was a leather satchel in the room, and Tommy took it, stuffing gadgets into it from his backpack, which he then stowed under one of the bunks.

They found the safe and extracted a thick wad of money from it.

The corridors of the bunker were heated by long metal

pipes that ran along the wall just above the floor. As they ascended the stairs out of the bunker, the temperature seemed to drop a degree for every step they took. Luke returned to Mueller's room and retrieved a couple of heavy woolen coats from the closet, along with mittens and hats. The hats were a strange woolen type with a peak, while the coats were brown, with black fur lining the collar.

Dressed more warmly, they left the bunker system and found their way up to the Hotel zum Türken.

The spacious and luxurious front drawing room was empty at that hour, and they settled down into a couple of overstuffed armchairs and waited for the first light.

At dawn, acting as if they had every right to be there—Tommy's first law of spying—they strolled down to the village to catch the alpine bus to Berchtesgaden town.

It had snowed overnight, and their feet crunched through a few inches of crisp white flakes as they walked into the village.

It was very different by daylight.

A huge, snow-covered mountain dominated the village, and not much farther away, a range of majestic alps punctured the skyline. Jutting out from a cliff top in the distance was a building perched right on the edge of the cliff. This was the famous Eagle's Nest, its concrete structures softened by thick snow.

They passed a huge, regal-looking house with grand pillars and archways, and he saw Tommy looking at it in wonder.

"That's the Berghof," Luke said. "Hitler's holiday house."

For some reason, that more than anything else brought

home to Luke where they were, *when* they were, and what they were doing there. They were standing outside the house of the evil tyrant who was responsible for World War II. The man who had conquered most of Europe but was eventually defeated by the combined might of the Allied forces.

If Mueller had his way and Hitler got the bomb, then his conquests would not stop at Europe. He would rule the world.

There were armed SS soldiers in a guardhouse that straddled the road up to the Berghof and the Hotel zum Türken. They were there to prevent people from getting in and were not worried about two Hitler Youths leaving the area. The guards waved them through with a quick glance, and Luke and Tommy headed down to the village to find a bus stop.

Smoke poured out through vents on the side of the bus, which was an old, unheated contraption that smelled of coal. It lurched precariously around corners that had only recently been plowed for snow, and Luke wondered if they would survive the trip to the railway station.

Their only companions on the bus were an old lady with a woolen head scarf and a wicker basket, and two soldiers in dress uniform, who sat at the back of the bus and did not give the Hitler Youths a second glance.

Luke dared not speak and just stared silently out of the grimy, smoke-stained windows at the houses they passed. He recognized some of them. The holiday homes of Martin Bormann, Hitler's private secretary; Hermann Göring, field marshal of the Luftwaffe (and Hitler's second in command); and Albert Speer, the Third Reich's head architect.

Tiny details from history books now took on a whole new significance.

A horse-drawn cart passed them, going up the hill as they went down. The horse looked young and strong, with big hooves and a shaggy mane. The driver by contrast was a withered old man, who seemed to be disappearing into a thick wool coat. The rear of the cart was packed with wooden crates and tall metallic cylinders that might have held milk.

Luke's stomach rumbled at that thought, and he realized that they hadn't eaten for hours.

The Bahnhof was a huge building with massive arched windows on the ground level and tall rectangular windows of crisscrossed panels that stretched up at least two more stories.

In front of the building, the long snout of an anti-aircraft gun pointed at the sky. Three soldiers were manning the gun, although they were currently resting against a wall of sandbags that surrounded it, drinking out of enamel mugs. Luke was aware of the soldiers' eyes upon them as they approached the Bahnhof. Was there something wrong with their clothes or haircuts? Thankfully, he and Tommy both had short hair, which wasn't too different from the short back and sides of other youths they saw.

He tried not to look at them.

The soldiers kept their eyes on them but did nothing as Luke and Tommy passed. Luke risked a quick glance back and saw that the gunners were still sitting, staring at other passersby.

By the main entrance, they passed a large statue of a soldier riding a horse.

Tommy saw Luke looking at it and whispered, "Where're a roll of toilet paper and duct tape when you need them?"

It was the first and last time Luke laughed that day.

The station was crowded, and at least half of the people seemed to be in a military uniform of some kind. He sat on a railway bench and avoided anyone's eyes, while Tommy went to book them into a private compartment on the train. They could afford it, and they both agreed it would be safer, as there would be fewer opportunities for Luke to reveal his lack of German.

While he was waiting, a small girl in a thick red wool coat wandered up to him, peering curiously at his bandages. There was fur around her collar and on her mittens. She was clutching a battered rag doll.

"Was ist los mit dir?" she asked, wide-eyed.

Luke shook his head and pointed to the bandages, hoping that Tommy would be back quickly.

"Was is los mit dir?" the girl asked again.

Luke looked away, hoping she would lose interest. A young couple on a nearby bench were watching curiously. *What was the girl asking him?* Should he just nod his head? Or shake it? Would either of those give him away? Would doing nothing be a signal to those around him that he was an imposter, a spy, an outsider in this world?

"Was ist los mit dir?" the girl asked for a third time, and

a man in a leather trench coat standing by the railway track was also now starting to take interest.

Luke shifted forward slightly on the seat, getting ready to make a run for it.

The man in the trench coat took a step in his direction.

Just at that moment, a woman approached, grabbed the girl's hand with some furious words, and hauled her away with an apologetic glance at Luke.

Luke risked a glance at the man in the leather trench coat to see him smile and wave at someone by the entrance just as Tommy arrived back with the tickets.

A counter near the ticket office sold them thick cheese sandwiches and large red apples that gradually quieted the gurgling coming from Luke's stomach. They bought extras, stored in a brown paper bag, in case they needed them for the journey.

They had not yet seen Mueller and his thugs, but the train did not leave until midday, so Luke expected them to arrive closer to that time, and he was right.

Luke and Tommy kept a discreet distance, always staying out of sight behind pillars or people as Mueller purchased tickets. Tommy had a coin in his hand and was passing the time with a simple game of flipping and catching it. They tried not to talk, in case someone should overhear them.

At first Tommy and Luke heard just a rumble in the distance and saw what looked like a low, small fog rolling in from the west above the trees. As it got closer, the fog became a dense cloud, and as the train rounded a long looping bend behind a wall of snow-covered trees, it became clear that they were watching snow flying up from either side of the train.

The train pulled up to the platform at exactly eleven-thirty, the massive brow of a snowplow leading the way. A huge wedge at the bottom of the plow lifted the snow, and a curved shield at the top hurled it out to either side of the train, creating the cloud they had seen.

There was nowhere for the train to turn around, and the tracks ended not far past the station, so Luke figured that there must be another engine at the other end of the train.

They waited for Mueller's group to board but were not far behind him, wanting to get to their compartment before Mueller was seated.

Mueller and his thugs boarded just one carriage in front of Luke and Tommy. Uncomfortably close, Luke felt, but maybe to their advantage, considering why they were on the train in the first place.

At five minutes before twelve, there was a commotion from the Bahnhof and a heavy black car pulled up outside. A figure emerged from one of the cars and entered the station, followed by an army officer carrying a briefcase. He made his way to the train and glanced up at their carriage as he approached.

The man smiled at Luke sympathetically, perhaps because of the bandages covering Luke's head, then disappeared into a carriage near the front of the train.

"Who do you think that was?" Tommy asked. "Himmler or Göring?"

"That was . . . Helmut Fricke," Luke said, mentally flicking through the pages of one of the books he had seen in the library. "He's an architect. Works for Albert Speer."

At exactly twelve, with a roaring, hissing sound and a grinding noise from underneath the train, they began to move. There was an initial jolt, then a growing sensation of speed as the station disappeared past their window, followed by the snow-covered mounds of trees.

In the distance, the beautiful white-capped mountains that watched over Berchtesgaden seemed to watch over Luke and Tommy as well.

Watching over? Or just watching?

In this strange land, full of strange people who spoke a strange language, Luke felt as alien as if he had come down in a spaceship from Mars. The slightest wrong move or overheard comment and they were lost. Captured by the police—or worse, the Gestapo.

Luke had read about a British prisoner of war who escaped and was recaptured when a German police officer noticed him looking the wrong way when crossing the road.

Such a simple thing, but it cost him his freedom.

For Luke and Tommy, every action, every gesture, every word needed to be above suspicion, and in Luke's case, that meant no words at all when German ears were listening.

Fields, softly blanketed with white, flew past the windows of the carriage. Luke turned to Tommy, and in low voices, they began to make plans.

32. POWERFUL MAGIC

A man in a gray uniform pushed open the door of their compartment and spoke rapidly in German.

Luke looked at him blankly, waiting for Tommy to give him a clue.

Tommy spoke back to the man and pulled out his ticket. Luke held up his as well, and the conductor inspected them both before marking them with a thick pen. He handed each of their tickets back and asked Luke something.

Luke began to panic, with no idea what the question was. Tommy remained calm, though, and pointed to the bandages swathed around Luke's head.

He seemed satisfied with Tommy's explanation but held out his hand again. Tommy fished inside his coat for his ID papers. Luke handed his over also.

The conductor's eyes narrowed, and he looked from one to the other, then back again.

Behind him, a man in Gestapo uniform moved up, blocking the doorway.

The conductor seemed confused and was asking rapid-fire questions of Tommy. He answered calmly, although Luke saw he was beginning to sweat.

The dark shape of a pistol in a leather holster made a bulge on the hip of the Gestapo officer.

What was wrong? Something about the photo? Had Gerda made some kind of a mistake when filling in the information?

The Gestapo officer pushed the conductor to one side and stepped forward, snatching the ID papers away from him. The officer's eyes widened when he saw the shape of the wolf's hook, and he glanced quickly at Tommy and Luke before letting out a blast of steam at the conductor.

Luke didn't have to speak German to know that the conductor was getting a good tongue-lashing.

The Gestapo man passed their papers back and retreated with a curt nod and a click of his heels, pulling the door shut behind him.

"What was that all about?" Luke asked softly when he was sure they were out of earshot.

"A lowly conductor does not question Werewolves," Tommy said.

Their papers were powerful magic, it seemed, in this place and time.

33. ATTACKED

A rhythmical *thump, thump, thump* came from the rear of the train. It startled Luke, who had been dozing. His first thought was that something was wrong with the train, but they did not slow and, in fact, seemed to accelerate.

He pressed his face to the window, trying to locate the source of the sound.

He could see nothing, so he pushed the sliding window of the carriage open and leaned out and, despite the freezing blast of air, craned his neck around. Tommy did the same beside him.

The train was on a slight curve, and Luke could see back to the rear carriages. Just in front of the rear engine was a low flatbed truck that had been covered with tarpaulins when they boarded. It was not covered now. The thin snouts of twin anti-aircraft guns were pounding away at something unseen in the sky.

Luke scanned the sky, searching for the target. The sky was clear, with occasional patches of cloud, and in one of those patches he saw them. Three aircraft, flying so closely together it was as if their wingtips were joined with string.

Flashes were coming from their wings. They were firing their guns. He idly wondered what they were firing at.

"Get down!" he yelled with sudden realization.

He dived to the floor, rolling underneath the wooden seat. Tommy was a fraction slower but made it just as the window shattered above them and the wooden paneling of the compartment exploded in a series of splintered holes.

Tommy rolled underneath the seat opposite and flattened himself against the wall. The seats would be little protection, Luke realized, looking at the size of the shell holes in the opposite wall.

There was an explosion from near the front of the train, and the entire carriage rocked.

The sound of the aircraft roared over their heads, so close that it seemed they must have just about peeled the top off the train.

The strafing run over, Luke climbed out from underneath the seat. All the glass in the window was gone, and it crunched on the floor beneath his boots. A wintery blast of air hit him in the face.

He found the trio of planes again, far in front of the train, banking as they circled around for another run.

The guns at the rear of the train fired incessantly, and a heavy machine gun had opened up somewhere else. Luke could see bright tracers weaving a lazy, curving string of pearls toward the fighters.

A tracer wandered onto the fuselage of one of the planes, and it shuddered, smoke pouring out behind it, peeling off from the attack.

"Got him!" Luke shouted, then stopped. Whoever these fighter planes were, British, American, or Russian, they were on his side. He was shouting in English, he suddenly realized, and hoped that no one had heard him over the noise of the train, the guns, and the aircraft engines.

The other two planes continued straight in.

"Here they come again!" Luke said in a frightened whisper, rolling back under the seat.

The carriage shuddered again, but not so close this time, and there were screams, then silence from somewhere behind them.

Luke stood up, a little wobbly on his feet, and searched the sky again, but he could not spot the planes.

Each of the cannon-fire holes in the compartment was big enough to put his fist through, and he wondered how Mueller and his friends were getting on at the front of the train.

Perhaps the aircraft could do the job for them.

Luke couldn't count on that, though.

The train was slowing now, even as he spotted the planes, circling around for another attack.

"What's going on?" Tommy asked, peering out the window with him.

Luke risked a look forward, leaning out of the shattered

window. Ahead of them, in the side of a mountain, was the black mouth of a tunnel.

"They're going to stop the train in the tunnel," he said to Tommy. "Wait for the fighters to leave."

Luke crawled back under the seat as the planes lined up for one final run. "This might be our chance," he said.

34. GOGGLES

It was pitch-black inside the tunnel. The train was unlit, running under blackout conditions. Luke could not even see Tommy, who was on the floor on the other side of the compartment.

"Pass me the goggles," Luke said. "I'm going to see if I can steal the plans."

"Do you want me to come with you?" Tommy asked, pushing the night-vision goggles across the floor in the darkness. He didn't sound very enthusiastic.

"No," Luke said. "One person will make less noise than two. You stay here. I'll be back soon."

He said it with an air of confidence that he did not feel.

Where would Mueller have the briefcase? On his lap? That would make it impossible.

The black ink of the corridor turned to a bizarre green world of shapes and strange bright edges as he pulled the night-vision goggles down over his head and stepped out of the compartment.

A sudden flash of light, impossibly bright, appeared at the end of the corridor, and he ducked back inside, shutting the door as a conductor, waving a flashlight, called out something in German.

Remain calm, Luke guessed. *Stay in your compartments.* Something like that.

As soon as the man had passed, Luke crept back into the corridor and headed toward the front of the train.

Shattered glass crunched underfoot, and he did his best to avoid it.

The damage from the cannon fire was everywhere, and he hoped that not too many people had been injured, or killed. The shell holes were mostly quite high in the walls of the corridor, and he felt that if, like them, they had sought shelter under the seats, they would have been safe.

At the far end of the corridor were two doors. One to his right, for boarding the train, and one directly in front of him, which led to the next carriage. The door to the next carriage squeaked, but he was not concerned. As long as the conductor didn't come back, there was no one to hear.

He stepped out of the train onto the narrow metal platform that linked the two carriages, grateful that the train was not moving.

It was bitterly cold outside, and he cursed the Hitler Youth uniform with its short pants. The platform was icy, and he almost slipped as he stepped across to the door of the next carriage just a few feet away. Through the glass window of the door, he could see that the area inside was empty, so he twisted the handle. The door opened quietly.

He glanced up for a moment at the walls of the tunnel, but the goggles could make out only blackness. Even so, the walls seemed to press down on him, crushing and suffocating him, and he quickly moved into the next carriage.

In the middle of the carriage, a man emerged from one of the compartments, perhaps to locate the source of the noise of the door opening and shutting.

Luke froze, although it was obvious from the way the man fumbled around the walls that he was totally blind in this utter darkness. Luke could not see his face, but from the bulky build of the man, he felt sure this was Jumbo or Mumbo.

Luke remained motionless, scarcely breathing, until the man realized that it was fruitless to move about in the dark and returned to his compartment.

Luke advanced, walking on the balls of his feet, then rolling back onto his heels so there was no sound as his feet met the floor.

He heard low voices as he neared the compartment, and wished that Tommy had come along after all, to translate. Perhaps they were discussing the noise he had made. Perhaps they were waiting for him to arrive so they could grab him.

The door to the compartment was still open, and he sidled up, keeping his back to the far wall of the corridor.

Mueller was seated by the window, his briefcase by his foot, against the wall. Jumbo and Mumbo sat on the other seat.

Their conversation finished, and there were no suspicious glances aimed at the corridor, so he hoped that whatever they had been discussing, it was not him.

Luke could see them so clearly, if a little greenly through the goggles, that it was hard to imagine that they could not see him, standing just a foot or so away.

His heart was pounding, and he willed it to ease, for his breathing to remain calm and quiet.

He dropped to the floor and crawled on his hands and knees into the room, keeping as far as he could from the feet of Jumbo, who was closest to the door.

As soon as he was inside the room, inside the lion's den, he crawled underneath Mueller's seat.

They were not talking, but he could hear them breathing. He could hear every rustle as one of them moved on their seats.

Surely, they could hear him, too. The rustling of his clothing as he crawled.

Probably they could. But not being able to see him, nor suspecting he was there, they would assume that the sounds came from one of the others in the compartment.

Luke crawled behind Mueller's feet, hoping Mueller wouldn't feel a sudden urge to shift them backward, under the seat.

He reached out for the briefcase, and his hand closed on the buckle just as Mueller's hand reached down from above, checking that the briefcase was still there, still safe.

His hand landed on the briefcase a few inches from Luke's, and Luke snatched his hand away.

Satisfied, Mueller's hand disappeared upward, out of Luke's field of vision.

Now was the time, Luke knew. His best chance to grab the plans before Mueller decided to check the briefcase again.

It was not the same briefcase he had had in the hotel. That had been a modern type with metal spring catches. This was an old-fashioned satchel-type case.

Luke reached out again, undid the buckle, and then carefully lifted up the top of the case. Mueller's leg moved, and Luke froze for a second, but Mueller said and did nothing else.

He felt around inside the briefcase. His hand closed on a folder, and he slowly drew it out and placed it on the floor in front of him, confirming that it was the plans. He folded it and slid it into an inner pocket in his coat.

He reached back and slipped the strap of the briefcase back through the buckle, refastening it, then eased backward underneath the seat, toward the doorway.

But there were footsteps in the corridor outside, and the compartment filled with light. The conductor and his flashlight!

Luke was sure that Jumbo or Mumbo would see him crouched under the seat opposite them; they only had to glance down.

The conductor said something briefly, and Mueller made some kind of acknowledgment; then the light disappeared.

There was a high-pitched squeal from the hinges, then a click from the latch as the door to the corridor was shut.

Luke looked around in panic.

There was no way he could open that door without them hearing. He was trapped in the compartment.

And when the train emerged from the tunnel, Jumbo and Mumbo would see him.

He struggled to control his breathing.

There's a way out of this, he thought, although he couldn't see one. There had to be a way.

There was a sudden lurch, then another, and the train began to move.

35. EASY AS

Luke fought rising panic and tried to think clearly. There were only a few minutes left before the train built up speed and cleared the tunnel and no way for him to open the door without them hearing.

But the door had to be opened by somebody.

He shuffled quietly around underneath the seat so he was facing the door; then he reached out, raised his hand as high as he could, and knocked three times on the compartment door.

"Hallo," Mueller said. *"Hallo. Wer ist es?"*

Luke waited a moment, then rapped on the door again.

"Hallo?" Mueller queried, and when there was no response, he said, *"Guck mal, wer da ist."*

Jumbo, closest to the door, stood up, a pistol appearing in his hand. *"Wer ist da?"* he said loudly. He flung open the door, and it banged against the corridor wall outside.

Mumbo rose and stood in front of Mueller, like a bodyguard.

Jumbo groped blindly outside the doorway, but of course there was nobody there. He took a few steps into the corridor.

The gap behind him was barely enough for Luke to squeeze through, but it was all he had. He rolled out from under the seat, stood, and slid around behind Jumbo.

Jumbo turned around, inches from Luke's face.

Luke took a slow step backward, then almost fell forward into Jumbo as the train lurched again. He would have hit him, too, if Jumbo hadn't taken a quick step backward at the same time to keep his own balance.

Minutes, maybe seconds now, before they hit daylight.

Luke eased back down the corridor away from Jumbo. He paused at the far door, not wanting to open it and create a noise while Jumbo was still standing in the corridor.

Ahead, out of the window, he could see a faint light, the end of the tunnel approaching. The train was moving faster.

Finally, Jumbo gave up and stepped back into the compartment. Luke slid the door open, and a moment later he was back in the other carriage.

The conductor was in the middle of the carriage, moving away from him, and Luke scurried along behind him. He reached his own compartment just as the windows of the train filled with brilliant green light.

Exhausted, he pulled the goggles off and handed them back to Tommy.

"How'd it go?" Tommy asked.

"Easy as, bro," Luke said.

36. DEVASTATION

"Awesome, dude!" Tommy said, leafing through the plans in the folder. "What do we do with them?"

"Destroy them," Luke said.

"Yes, but how?"

Luke hadn't thought about that.

"We could burn them," Tommy suggested.

"You got a gadget for that, too?" Luke asked.

"Nope," Tommy said.

Luke pulled his overcoat tightly around him. With the window gone, the central heating of the train could do little to cope with the freezing air that was rushing in from outside.

The warmest place was on the floor, by the heating vents, and that was where they were both sitting, finishing off the extra sandwiches they had bought from the shop in Berchtesgaden.

"Whatever we do, we should do it soon," Tommy said. "In

case Mueller finds out the plans are missing and they search the train."

"We could eat them," said Luke.

They both looked at the thick sheaf of papers enclosed in the folder and shook their heads in unison, taking another bite of their sandwiches instead.

"We could dissolve them in acid," Tommy said. "If we had some acid."

"Yeah, and we could put them in a rocket and send them to the moon," Luke said. "If we had a moon rocket."

They batted back and forth various and increasingly silly ways to destroy the plans, but in the end all they did was rip them into small pieces, page by page, and release them out through the shattered window, the bits fluttering into the ice and the snow and the trees.

They scattered the plans over miles and miles of countryside, then tore the cardboard folder into pieces and did the same for that, laughing like maniacs the whole time.

They watched the outskirts of Munich slip by with a growing feeling of confidence and hope. Against the odds, their mission was accomplished. All they had to do now was return to Berchtesgaden. To go home.

The low, outlying buildings became taller as the train approached the center of the city. They passed beautiful white-brick buildings with steep orange roofs and tall spires. But Allied bombers had been through here, and as they continued on, the magnificent architecture gave way to fire-blackened ruins—houses collapsed in on themselves, buildings with entire front walls missing, allowing them to see into every rubble-strewn room.

In one area, there was not a single building standing, just jagged spears of brick and the remnants of walls rising piti-fully from mounds of debris around them. Whole suburbs had been ground into the dirt.

The smell of the city poured into the carriage through the shattered window. The reek of lingering smoke, dust, and decay mingled with a strong odor of disinfectant.

People were moving amid the destruction, digging in the rubble or hauling their possessions through the streets in handcarts or suitcases.

What looked like a family—two parents and three children—sat on two ragged sofas in the middle of the street outside a bombed-out building. Their faces, hair, and clothes were covered with gray dust. They sat, unmoving, waiting for something, or perhaps nothing at all.

A lush park, with playground equipment for kids, was untouched by the bombing but was now home to rows of roughly dug graves.

"It's like September eleventh, times a hundred," Tommy whispered beside him.

"Times a thousand," Luke said.

Luke's desire to leave this place—this nightmarish world—increased with every mile. He wanted to get back to the comfort and peace of the twenty-first century. Nothing in his experience could possibly have prepared him for the horrors that these people were going through, and he knew that it was far worse in many other countries.

He wanted desperately to go home.

But even before the train pulled to a halt at the railway station, the Ostbahnhof, they could see that something was terribly wrong.

37. A FACT

Passengers waiting to board were being herded away from the train. Long rows of soldiers were running up the platform's stairs. Gestapo officers in their black uniforms with the swastika on a bloodred armband were directing people into lines.

Guns were drawn.

"Is it us?" Tommy's face was white.

"I don't know," Luke replied, but thought it probably was. Mueller must have discovered the theft, and someone must have radioed ahead to the station.

The train stopped and settled with a hiss and clouds of smoke, and he saw Mueller exit the train and go speak to one of the Gestapo officers.

"Come on," Luke said. "We've got to get off this train before they start searching it."

They ran down to the exit door, hauled it open, and stopped dead on the steps.

On the platform, right in front of the door, were five soldiers in the field gray-green of the Wehrmacht, their rifles raised. A Gestapo officer stood beside them, his pistol leveled at Luke's face.

"Halt!" he yelled.

They halted, frozen to the steps. Tommy was so close behind Luke that he could feel his breath on the back of his neck.

Mueller appeared alongside the Gestapo man. His eyes were cold and still, like the air before a thunderstorm, and Luke could see that the storm was coming.

"Where are the plans?" he barked. "What have you done with them?"

"We destroyed them." Luke kept his voice steady, despite the guns. "It's over. The plans are gone."

"Stupid boys," Mueller snarled. "I will simply return and print out a new set."

"You'll find armed police waiting for you," Luke said, knowing it was not true. Ms. Sheck had promised not to leave the cave.

That shut Mueller up for a moment. His eyes—vicious, feral—twitched. Thinking. He said, "You drew those plans once from memory. You will do it again for us."

Luke's world stood still. How could he have been so stupid? He did know those plans. He could easily draw them again, and threatened with torture, he doubted that he would be able to resist.

If they had him, they had the atomic bomb.

But without him, they had nothing. They needed him alive.

"So shoot me," he yelled. "Go ahead, fire!" They wouldn't dare.

Luke stepped backward up the steps, pushing Tommy back with him, slamming the metal door of the carriage in front of him.

A shot rang out and glass sprayed all around them. He heard Mueller shouting from the platform, *"Nicht schießen! Nicht schießen!"*

They ran back along the corridor, crouching low so they couldn't be seen.

One of the corridor windows had been shattered by the airplane attack, and Luke rushed at it. He slipped off a shoe and used it to smash away the remains of the broken glass on the bottom edge before climbing through and lowering himself to the tracks.

On the other side of the train, the platform side, he could hear shouting.

Tommy emerged from the window and fell onto him, knocking them both down just as boots sounded in the corridor.

"Quick!" Luke said, and they crawled beneath the massive metal wheels of the carriage into the space underneath.

Forward or backward? They had to move. Mueller's men would quickly figure out what they had done.

Luke chose forward, operating on that strange intuition that tells you the right thing to do even while your mind is still trying to work it out.

They crawled beneath one, then another carriage, shielded from view by the height of the platform to their left.

There was something different about the next carriage. It was cleaner. Luke could see a glimpse of the rear wall as they scuttled underneath the linking platform; it was polished and brass.

It was the VIP carriage. The one reserved for officials of the Nazi party.

Then it came to him.

Three lines out of one of the books he had read in the library.

One piece of information.

A single fact.

But it could save their lives.

Luke risked a look over the edge of the linking platform. The attention was still on the other end of the train.

"Follow me!" he said, and climbed up onto the linking platform between the carriages.

The handle of the door appeared to be made of gold, and embossed in the glass window of the door was a large swastika. Luke grabbed the handle, opened the door, and stepped into the corridor.

Tommy shut the door behind them. Again they kept low. As they got to each compartment, Luke popped his head up to see if it was occupied.

The first three were not. The last one was.

Luke stepped inside as the man in the compartment looked up, startled. He had a large notebook in one hand and a pen in the other, although he placed the pen down as they entered. He wore a dark brown civilian suit. Tommy closed the door, and Luke sank into the plush leather chair opposite the man.

Tommy sat in the chair beside Luke.

The man looked at the two boys without alarm. Luke glanced quickly at Tommy and said in English, "Helmut Fricke, three months from now in the Reich Chancellery in Berlin, you are going to attempt to assassinate Adolf Hitler."

38. THE GOOD MAN

Fricke's expression did not change.

"You are British," he said in perfect, although accented, English.

"From New Zealand," Luke said, slowly unwrapping the bandages from around his head. No longer any need to pretend.

Fricke smiled. "Young man, I think we are at war with your country. Should I be afraid?"

Luke shook his head but said nothing.

"Assassinate the Führer? In the chancellery?" he asked, and his eyes flicked once to the door. "Who would tell you such a thing about me?"

"I read it in a book," Luke said.

"A book." He tapped the end of his pen on his notepad. "A novel, of course. Or propaganda from the British or Americans."

"Neither," Luke said. "It was a history book." He gave

that time to sink in, then continued. "In February, you and the man you work for, Albert Speer, will decide that the Führer is committing high treason against the German people. Perhaps you have decided that already."

"Hitler? High treason?" Fricke's expression was not yet one of anger, but it was getting close.

"Yes," Luke continued. "You will see in the chancellery gardens a ventilation shaft that leads to Hitler's bunker. You and Mr. Speer will ask a man named Stohl, or Stahl, I think—"

"Dieter Stahl?"

"Yes. You will ask him for some new nerve agent called Tabun, with the idea of somehow pouring it down the ventilation shaft. But he will tell you that it won't work, and then armed guards will be placed on the shafts, which stops the whole idea."

"This is preposterous," Fricke said, his voice raised, and turned toward the door of the compartment.

"Don't worry—Hitler will never learn of the plot," Luke said.

Fricke opened his mouth to call out.

"Your son will grow up to be a highly respected scientist," Luke said desperately, scratching for anything else he could remember from the books. "He will move to America and become one of the team that will land mankind on the moon."

Fricke closed his mouth abruptly.

"Man on the moon?" he said, raising an eyebrow in clear disbelief.

"It's true," Tommy said.

"I don't even have a son," Fricke said.

"Yes, you do!" Luke said. "It's a recorded fact. He was born on . . ." His voice trailed off. "May eighth, 1945. The same day the war ended."

Crap! That was still months away. What else did he know about Helmut Fricke? He shut his eyes, visualizing the pages of the books he had read. But there was nothing that seemed to help.

He opened his eyes again, expecting the worst, but he was surprised to see only a look of confusion on Fricke's face.

"A son," Fricke said, a wisp of a smile playing at the corners of his mouth. "My wife is with child. The baby is expected in early May. But you could not know these things! We have told no one." The anger in his voice was gone.

Luke looked him in the eye and said, "You will survive the war. Afterward, you will be charged with war crimes but eventually cleared of any wrongdoing."

"I don't know how you could imagine these things," Fricke said.

"I told you, I read them in a book."

"A history book? This book must have come from the future."

"Mr. Fricke," Tommy said, "*we* have come from the future."

There was a knock on the door of the compartment, and a soldier slid the door open, peering suspiciously at the two boys.

Luke held his breath and felt Tommy draw back on the seat beside him.

"My nephews from Munich," Fricke said. "They're not the boys you are looking for."

The soldier left with a quick "Heil Hitler."

Fricke sat in deep thought, looking at them. He was a tall man, with blond hair and an air of authority in his speech and manner.

Everything now depended on his believing this outrageous, incredible story. A story that even Luke himself was having trouble believing.

But Fricke nodded and said after a while, almost to himself, *"Das Vitruvian Projekt."*

Luke's jaw dropped.

Tommy asked, "You know about the Vitruvian chamber?"

Fricke said, "Only a little, and only because Herr Speer was asked to help design a magnetic shield wall for the chamber and sought my advice on some matters. All I really know is that something was found. Something very secret. Something very old. I heard it was in catacombs under a monastery in Florence. I believe we have agents scouring the world for some drawings, which are missing."

He thought for a moment longer, then said, "Imagine if I was to believe you. Imagine if I was to tell you that I have had discussions with Herr Stahl and Herr Speer along the lines you suggest and that nobody else could have known this. That would put me at great risk, especially if your story turns out to be a clever ruse by the Gestapo."

"It's not," Luke said.

"And what you have not explained is what you are doing here, and why everyone is looking for you," Fricke said.

"A man named Erich Mueller used the Vitruvian Project"—Luke borrowed Fricke's term for it—"to bring back plans from the future for a weapon so powerful that it will change the course of the war. We followed him here to try and stop him."

"And you want my help? But I am German—perhaps you noticed. Should I not hope that Germany would win the war?"

"The weapon is an atomic bomb," Tommy said. "One bomb can wipe out a city. It will be a disaster."

"The Americans already have the same weapon, and if Hitler has it, too, there will be a nuclear war," Luke said. "It will be like the Blitz in London, only a hundred times worse. This will condemn millions of people to death, for nothing."

Fricke looked at Tommy, then back at Luke. "The 'Blitz'? This is the German word for *lightning*. What do you mean by it? What is the Blitz in London?"

Luke frowned. Surely Fricke knew about the Blitz. He said, "The bombing of London in 1940. It was known as the Blitz."

"The Blitz." Fricke said it slowly. "A good word for a terrible tragedy. We have had the same kind of 'Blitz' in Berlin, and even worse in Cologne. Did you know?"

Luke nodded.

Fricke tapped his fingers on the seat beside him. "Does the Führer now have these plans?"

"No, we destroyed them."

"Then the problem has gone, yes?"

"Not quite," Luke said. "There is one more copy of the plans." He tapped his head. "In here."

For some reason, sitting down with Helmut Fricke, calmly discussing the situation instead of running and hiding and dodging bullets and the Gestapo, brought the reality crashing down on Luke with a thump, and he paled.

Fricke said, "Are you all right?"

"I'm okay," Luke said. "But it just kind of hit home that if Mueller and your Führer get hold of me, then . . ." He trailed off, unable to bring himself to say what had to be said next.

Fricke waited, and Tommy stared at him with concern.

Luke looked at Tommy, right into the eyes of his best mate in the world, and said, "If we can't get back to the chamber, if we can't escape from Mueller, then I have to die. And you may have to do it."

"No way, dude. That's crazy," Tommy said.

"Is it?" Luke asked. "If I live, and they catch me, then I will be responsible for a nuclear holocaust. That can't be allowed to happen."

"What is it that you would like me to do?" Fricke asked. "Assuming that I believe you."

"My only chance—our only chance—is to get back to Berchtesgaden," Luke said. "Back to the bunker and the Vitruvian chamber."

"Back home. Back to . . . ?"

"The twenty-first century," Luke said.

He whistled softly. "A new millennium. A different world, I think."

"Very," Tommy agreed.

Fricke looked from one of them to the other, undecided.

He said, "You found my name in a history book."

"Yes," Luke said.

"History. How will it remember me?"

"As one of the few who stood up to Hitler," Luke said. "As a good man."

Fricke nodded and seemed to sit up a little straighter in his chair.

There was a knock on the door.

"Herein bitte," he called, and a young officer entered.

His eyes flicked over them and settled back on Fricke.

"Herr Mueller möchte Sie sprechen," he said.

Luke didn't need to speak German to catch the name Mueller.

"Ja, er soll reinkommen," Fricke replied, and when the door closed, he said, "Perhaps you boys might like to make yourselves invisible for a moment." He indicated a small door to one side of the compartment. Luke opened it to find a closet, just large enough for him and Tommy. It was empty except for Fricke's overcoat. They scrambled inside, Luke thinking clearly enough to snatch up the discarded bandages as he did so.

A moment later there was another knock. The officer was back. They heard Mueller's voice as well.

Fricke did not invite him to sit.

Fricke and Mueller spoke in German, but Tommy translated it for Luke, whispering into his ear as the men talked. Mueller was telling Fricke a cock-and-bull story about Luke and Tommy being British spies, trained to infiltrate Germany, as they wouldn't be suspected because of their age.

Fricke said he had not seen them.

Mueller apologized for the inconvenience and for the delay while the train was being searched.

Fricke accepted his apology, then said, "Perhaps it is for the best. After the blitz last night in Berlin, I am not in such a hurry to return."

"It was terrible," Mueller agreed. "The British are indiscriminate with their bombing."

"It is true," Fricke said, then continued in a different tone. "You were not injured earlier, when the train was strafed?"

"Fortunately not," Mueller said. "And you and your men?"

"This carriage is armored," Fricke said. "But I fear the strafing is my fault. This carriage is a magnet for enemy aircraft."

"The tunnel was a stroke of fortune, then."

"Indeed."

"I must now return to Berchtesgaden," Mueller said.

Inside the closet, Luke froze. Mueller's heading back to Berchtesgaden could mean only one thing. He was planning to go back through the time chamber to get another set of the plans. Ms. Sheck would be there, waiting, as Luke had insisted.

And Mueller would let nothing stand in his way.

"So soon?" Fricke asked.

"Yes. Some important business has come up. I would be honored if you would allow me to use your carriage."

Don't let him! Luke willed Fricke to say no.

"My apologies, Herr Mueller, but I am not permitted to let anyone use the carriage," Fricke said.

"I understand, Herr Fricke, but perhaps this will persuade you."

Even without seeing it, Luke could guess what Mueller was showing Fricke. His Werewolf identity card. Powerful magic.

"I did not realize, and I wish I could oblige. However, I myself do not have the authority to—"

"Herr Fricke, need I remind you that the Führer himself said that Werewolves are to be afforded every assistance?"

"Yes, but—"

Fricke was trying his best not to let Mueller use his compartment with Luke and Tommy stuck in the closet. But clearly he was not going to win.

"Every assistance. Perhaps we should telephone Herr Speer for authority."

"There is no need. I will get my coat," Fricke said.

The door to the closet opened, just enough for Fricke to retrieve his overcoat. He mouthed *Sorry* before shutting the door again.

The closet was barely big enough for the two of them, and Luke was very conscious that the slightest noise would lead to their discovery. He couldn't imagine how they were going to remain hidden for the whole journey back to Berchtesgaden.

A few minutes after Fricke left, there was a knock on the door and Luke heard Jumbo's and Mumbo's voices as they entered the compartment. He prayed that none of them would decide to check the closet.

It took at least half an hour before the searchers decided that the two hunted boys were not on the train, and released it for its return trip to Berchtesgaden.

There was some movement after a while, and Luke guessed that they were removing some of the more damaged carriages and replacing them with new ones. He and Tommy braced themselves against the sides of the closet as best they could. It would be a disaster if the train jolted suddenly and they burst out of the closet door right under the nose of their hunters.

Eventually, the train began to move and gather speed. It was a curse and a blessing. A curse because the rocking meant constantly bracing themselves this way and that. After just ten minutes, Luke's arms and legs were aching. But it was a blessing because the noise of the train covered any small sounds they made.

Still, it was with great relief that he finally felt the train begin to slow as it pulled into Berchtesgaden.

39. CORKS

The big wheels of the locomotive came to a final, shuddering halt, the metallic squeals and grinding of the carriage contrasting with the delicate tinkling of the chandelier in the compartment.

They waited for the three men to leave before inching open the closet door.

"What now?" Tommy asked. "Try and get clear of the station before he spots us? Or wait till he's gone?"

"I'm not sure," Luke said. "We have to beat him back to the chamber, but we can't risk being seen."

A moment later, the question was out of their hands. A low siren sounded somewhere near the station, a loud whining that grew even louder and higher in pitch.

Luke peeked through the curtains to see the platform was in pandemonium, with people running in all directions. Some dropped their suitcases where they were standing; others ran with them, using them as battering rams to barge through the crowds.

Tommy looked at Luke, and Luke looked back, both uncertain what to do.

"Let's go," Luke said at last. "We can mingle with the crowds so Mueller doesn't see us. If we can stay out of his way in the air-raid shelter, then we can try and beat him up the hill to Obersalzberg."

Luke peered out from the doorway before stepping down onto the platform. Mueller was nowhere to be seen.

He scanned the faces in the crowd, all of them panicked and hurried, making for the exits as quickly as the crush of bodies would let them.

No Mueller. No Mumbo or Jumbo. Time to go.

"Stay frosty," he said, then jumped down and waited for Tommy to land beside him before pushing into the thick of the crowd.

A soldier at one of the exits was handing out something to the crowd. Some took it; some didn't. As Luke approached, he saw the soldier was giving away corks from wine bottles. He took one, as did Tommy, but they must have looked confused, because the soldier mimed putting the cork between his teeth and said something in German.

"You put it in your mouth," Tommy told him as they emerged from the Bahnhof into the sunshine outside. "Between your teeth, for the percussion."

Luke guessed it acted a bit like a mouth guard.

Outside, Luke looked up at the clear blue sky, expecting to find it darkened with the black shapes of bombers, but there were none.

The soldiers manning the anti-aircraft gun were at their posts, searching the skies, but the gun was stationary.

Perhaps it was a false alarm.

Perhaps not.

People abandoned cars in the middle of the road, leaving doors wide open as they ran for the shelters.

As Luke and Tommy hurried along with the crowd, a motorcycle and sidecar swerved violently up to the footpath. The rider and his passenger jumped out and dashed along the road in front of them.

The stream of people poured across the road, disappearing into a big stone building with a large sign on the front: LUFTSCHUTZBUNKER. That had to be the shelter.

Luke and Tommy ran with the crowd, breathless, frightened, sweating despite the cold. Around them the siren filled the air, rising and falling in a horrible moaning sound. In the distance, Luke could see some dark dots that had to be aircraft.

Tommy stopped suddenly in his tracks. "Danger close. Twelve o'clock," he said in a low voice.

Luke's eyes left the sky and landed on the back of the head of the person in front of him.

It was a man in uniform.

An SS uniform.

There was something about the build and the shape of the neck that made his spine shudder, and even before the man turned around, Luke knew who it was

Then he did turn around.

Jumbo's eyes widened, and he stopped dead.

He shouted in German, and Luke saw Mueller and Mumbo stop and turn also.

"Oh, crap!" Tommy said.

Tommy and Luke turned and ran, ducking and weaving through the crowd.

There was more shouting from behind them, and Luke looked back. Jumbo and Mumbo were using their bulk to barge people out of the way.

Somehow they dodged through the flow of human traffic, and the first thing Luke saw as they emerged into the open was the motorcycle and sidecar parked haphazardly against the footpath.

"Get in!" Luke yelled, leaping over the motorcycle frame.

"Can you drive one of these things?" Tommy shouted over the scream of the siren, and jumped into the sidecar.

"Let's find out!" Luke shouted back. It couldn't be too different from the quad bike he used to ride on the farm.

He stood on the kick-starter, and the engine, still warm, revved and caught. He toed it into gear and let the clutch out. The bike jerked, jolted forward, and stalled.

Jumbo and Mumbo were free of the crowd now and were running after them, pistols raised.

Luke kicked the starter again, and the bike roared to life. He eased out the clutch, and the back wheel spun but then gripped, and the bike shot off.

He twisted the handlebars around, and the bike slewed away from Jumbo and Mumbo. There were shots now, and he could hear a zinging noise as bullets punched holes in the air around them.

Then they were moving down the main road of Berchtesgaden. Luke swerved the bike from side to side, hoping to spoil their aim, throwing Tommy around in the sidecar. Tommy gripped the sides with clawed hands and looked behind with terror in his eyes.

The roads were still icy, and mounds of snow were piled up around telegraph poles and in snow hedges along the pavement where the plows had been at work that morning.

Luke spun the bike around the corner toward Obersalzberg and glanced back to see a black open-top German army staff car pull out after them. Jumbo was driving, with Mumbo next to him and Mueller in the rear.

Mumbo had acquired a machine gun, and he let off a long burst, which was terrifying, although the bullets came nowhere near them, his aim thrown off by the motion of the car.

The sun was blotted out for a moment, and Luke glanced up to see not clouds but the long dark shape of airplane after airplane droning overhead.

The anti-aircraft gun was shooting now, spitting fire into the sky, each recoil raising a cloud of dust around it.

He expected bombs, but there were none, and that was when he realized with sheer and utter horror what their target was.

The Allied bombers had no interest in Berchtesgaden, a sleepy little Bavarian alpine town.

They were after the Nazi party stronghold, and perhaps Hitler's Eagle's Nest, at Obersalzberg.

Right where Luke and Tommy were headed.

40. THE JAWS OF DEATH

Luke slid the back wheel of the heavy motorbike around a corner, the bike skidding toward a snowdrift and a sheer drop beyond.

The handlebars shuddered in his hands as he fought to control the machine, which behaved almost nothing like his quad bike back home.

The car slid around the same tight corner, not far behind them, and Jumbo let loose another burst of wild machine-gun fire.

Luke looked at Tommy to make sure he was okay and got a quick thumbs-up. He had his cork clenched firmly between his teeth. Luke had forgotten about his, so when they hit a straight stretch, he fished it out of his pocket and jammed it into his mouth.

Lightning flashed ahead of them and thunder rumbled— only, Luke knew it was neither lightning nor thunder. A blast of air buffeted the bike.

There were more explosions, closer now, massive fists of wind that knocked the bike around the road. He leaned low over the handlebars, urging the machine forward. The explosions were a continuous roar as tons of high explosives hit the mountainside over Obersalzberg.

And they were heading into the heart of it.

There was a flash on the mountainside above them, and a cloud of snow erupted above their heads. Huge splinters of wood, entire branches and pulverized tree trunks, flew through the air.

One massive chunk of wood landed on the road, and Luke swerved madly up onto the embankment to get around it, hoping it might create a roadblock for the staff car behind them. But when he looked back, it was still on their tail.

Even more explosions, lifting whole trees up by their roots and spinning them into the air.

The bike heaved and bucked, and he hung on grimly as snow and smoke filled the road. Any sharp corners ahead and they would be toast. Luke could see no more than ten feet in front of his face.

The cloud cleared and he was staring at a paper-thin wooden barrier guarding the edge of a sheer drop. He yelled and twisted the handlebars, swinging the machine around. It slipped and skidded but turned, the sidecar scraping along the barrier, avoiding the cliff face by a few shavings of wood.

The road straightened out into the center of Obersalzberg.

It was smoother here, too, which made for easier going,

but Luke realized suddenly that it also made it easier for Jumbo to aim.

The zinging sound of bullets flying past his head was only slightly less terrifying than the enormous shattering crump of the explosions around them.

"I thought he wanted you alive!" Tommy yelled.

"Not anymore!" Luke yelled back.

If they could beat Mueller back to the chamber, they could go through it and change the settings, trapping Mueller in the past.

Mueller must have realized that, too.

The guardhouse ahead was deserted. It did not seem to have been hit, but it was on fire, perhaps from hot shrapnel.

He saw the Berghof, Hitler's luxurious alpine mansion, take a direct hit, wood and stone spewing into the air in a horrifying volcano of masonry and smoke. Incredibly, he saw a toilet, completely intact, come flying up out of the eruption. It somersaulted end over end and disappeared somewhere in the woods behind the house.

He glanced upward again and was shocked to see the planes still coming, wave after wave of them.

The sky filled with swarms of small black insects, flying in jagged lines—only, they weren't insects; they were bombs falling from the aircraft above.

The mountains around them were dancing, and the god of thunder was clapping his hands and stamping his feet to keep time.

It seemed incredible that anything or anyone would be able to survive the obliteration that was happening before their eyes. No sane person would keep going, but if Mueller caught them, it was the end of everything.

Luke gunned the bike up the road that led to the now-ruined Berghof, and the Hotel zum Türken beyond that.

They hit the corner on just two wheels, the sidecar lifting off the ground, and that was the position they were in when the bomb hit close by.

The entire motorcycle was hauled from the ground by a huge, hot balloon of air and debris and was thrown sideways as if it were just a cheap plastic toy. Luke lost his grip on the handlebars and tumbled through the air, seeing the edge of the drainage ditch drift past in slow motion, then the far edge approach. Then nothing but blackness.

He was conscious. He was alive. At least he thought he was. There wouldn't be so much pain if he were dead.

His ribs were on fire, and one of his legs was throbbing with stabbing spikes of pain that shot through his whole body.

The ground beneath him was bucking and heaving, the ditch shaking like jelly as explosion after explosion pounded around him.

He couldn't breathe. His throat was blocked, and when he tried to suck in air, there was just a high-pitched croaking sound. His hand flew to his throat. Was his neck injured? His windpipe crushed?

He managed a gasping, choking cough, and something shot into his mouth and his airway cleared.

Luke sucked in a chestful of horrible, bitter air, filled with acrid smoke and cordite, but it tasted better than the purest mountain air. Then he spat the object out of his mouth and onto the ground. It was the cork. Or rather, half the cork.

Tommy!

Was he alive or dead?

Luke forced himself to roll over onto his stomach and pressed upward with his arms.

He could see the crushed shape of the motorcycle ahead and crawled toward it, ignoring the pain in his legs and ribs. He squeezed between the edge of the ditch and the bike and found Tommy, half in and half out of the sidecar. He'd somehow stayed in it as it was blasted off the road.

Tommy's face was covered in blood and mud, and his clothing was torn and blackened. Blood was flowing out of a wound on his scalp, and Luke feared he was dead, but as he touched Tommy's leg, he opened his eyes.

"Dude, you look awful," Tommy said.

There was another string of explosions, and although they sounded farther away, Luke pressed himself to the bottom of the ditch, realizing that it was probably this ditch that had saved their lives as the mountainside had been ripped apart around them.

Then there was silence.

Utter silence.

The bombing had stopped.

No birds chirped in the trees, and no wind whispered around the mountainside. Nothing dared disturb this eerie calmness.

"I think it's over," Luke said. "Can you walk?"

"Yes." Tommy nodded. "But can you?"

Luke looked down to see his right kneesock was no longer white but bright red. He pulled himself to his feet, using the remains of the bike for leverage, and carefully put weight on his leg.

It hurt like hell, but it held his weight. It wasn't broken at least.

"I can walk," Luke said, but Tommy wasn't listening. He was looking back down the hillside toward the intersection and the road to Berchtesgaden.

"But can you run?" Tommy asked.

Luke followed his gaze and saw Mueller and Mumbo emerge through swirling clouds of smoke, automatic weapons in their arms.

41. THE MOUTH OF HELL

Tommy rolled up and out of the far side of the ditch and reached back down for Luke.

"Run!" Luke shouted at him. "Get back to the bunker."

"Get a grip, dude," Tommy said. He grabbed Luke's arm and hauled him up out of the ditch.

Mueller lifted his gun, and bullets smacked into the trunks of the trees behind them.

"Come on!" Tommy yelled, putting one of Luke's arms around his shoulders.

As Luke ran, he thought it was amazing what the human body could do when there was a madman with a machine gun behind you.

They staggered, stumbled, and lurched into the small forest behind them. When they had seen it that morning, it had been a proud stand of fir trees, tall with a fine head of snow. Now the snow was gone, shaken from the branches by the pounding of the explosions. So were many of the trees, grotesquely twisted and distorted into a maze of splintered wood.

Smoke swirled through the small forest, making ghastly, ghostly shapes of the maimed trees. White smoke and dirty gray smoke intermingled in strange scything patterns.

But there were no colors in this landscape; everything was burned black or ash white or smoky shades of gray.

Mueller and Mumbo disappeared, but Luke knew they were not far away.

"Not in a straight line," Luke whispered.

They zigzagged a random course through the forest, but always uphill, knowing that sooner or later that would take them to the hotel. As they moved, they listened for any sound that might help them locate Mueller and Mumbo, while at the same time trying to make as little sound themselves as possible.

What about Jumbo? Luke wondered. Was he also somewhere in the misty smoke, hunting for them? Or was he lying injured in the remains of the car?

The clouds of smoke, dust, and pulverized concrete drifted and swirled, sometimes smothering them in a thick blanket and other times clearing almost to nothing. The smoke crept into their nostrils and mouths, tasting like a spoonful of hot ash.

A crumpled, twisted mess of timber and masonry appeared out of nowhere in one of the strange hollows in the clouds. Only the fancy terrace on the far side allowed him to recognize it as the ruins of the Berghof. The fuming wreckage of Hitler's holiday home was perhaps a symbol of what lay in store for his empire, his Third Reich.

They skirted around a huge bomb crater rimmed with the splintered skeletons of trees, and emerged into a natural clearing.

In the center, motionless, stood a fawn. It watched them approach, blinking, but didn't run.

As they passed it, Luke reached out a hand and ran it along the back of the creature, feeling the fine fur rub like velvet against his fingers. The fawn did not flinch.

A burst of machine-gun fire sounded as they got to the trees at the far side of the clearing, Mueller or Mumbo shooting at shadows. Luke glanced back at the fawn, but it remained motionless, a statue. He watched it until it disappeared from sight.

Tommy stopped suddenly and put a hand over Luke's mouth.

Mueller and Mumbo appeared from behind a crisscross of fallen trees in front of them, heading uphill.

Mumbo started to turn, to look back at them, but just as he did, a cloud of smoke and dust grasped him in swirling gray fingers and he faded from sight, despite being only a few yards away.

Luke and Tommy struck out at a right angle, trying to put distance between them. They were not far from the hotel now, and he strove to move faster, to be less of a burden to Tommy. Tommy was uncomplaining. Taking half of Luke's weight, he strode forward tirelessly.

They almost stumbled over Hitler's toilet. It had landed

upright, wedged between a tree and a fallen trunk. It was cracked but otherwise intact.

The seat was up and Luke thought, a little insanely, that his mother would not approve of that. *You might as well spray crap all around the room.*

They neared the top of the road, and still he could not see the hotel. Then he realized they were looking at it. Half of it, anyway. The other half was gone. Another direct hit.

The Allies had pasted this area, obliterating the holiday resort of the hated Nazis, and he cheered them for it, even as he cursed them for it.

They stumbled to the hotel and picked a way inside, over broken timber and furniture that had been tossed around the front room.

There was another loud burst of machine-gun fire behind them. Plaster flew in puffs from the walls, and a mirror on the far wall, somehow still intact, shattered and fell.

They ducked and Luke looked back to see Mueller and Mumbo closing in on the hotel.

"Hurry," Tommy said.

Mumbo fired again as they stumbled deeper into the ruin. The staircase down to the bunker was undamaged, and they pretty much fell down it, dragging themselves back to their feet at the bottom.

The large metal door that led into the complex was shut, and when Luke tried the handle, he found it was locked.

Above they could hear Mueller and Mumbo moving through the rubble on the first floor.

Tommy banged desperately on the door, and to Luke's amazement, there was a click, and it opened an inch.

An eye peered out, but when it saw two boys, bruised, battered, in ragged Hitler Youth uniforms, the door sprung open.

The man at the door was a tall SS officer with a black patch over one eye and a jagged scar that ran from his ear to his chin. He moved aside to let them in.

A few more SS men were in the corridor, all armed with pistols or automatic weapons. Other eyes watched them from the doorways that lined the corridor.

There were footsteps on the stairs behind them.

Luke, still leaning on Tommy's shoulder, put his mouth to Tommy's ear and whispered, "American soldiers."

Tommy caught on at once. *"Amerikanische Soldaten!"* he shouted, pointing behind them at the stairs. *"Amerikanische Soldaten!"*

Luke couldn't imagine what American soldiers would be doing advancing through Obersalzberg in the middle of an air raid, but it was enough to panic the SS troops.

The first man slammed the big metal door and flicked shut the catches on all four corners. Luke and Tommy were bustled away from the entrance, and the SS took defensive positions in the corridor, training their weapons on the door. From the nursing station, a woman beckoned to Luke and Tommy, but they didn't have time for that. Luke shook his head and gestured down the corridor as if they had somewhere they needed to be.

Which they did.

They heard a banging on the door behind them and shouts muffled by the metal.

The SS troops would be suspicious, suspecting a trick by the "American soldiers" outside, but it wouldn't take Mueller long to convince them.

They walked as quickly as they could past the dim doorways and the frightened eyes that peered out from each room, trying not to look like they were running.

Inside the bunker, the going was easier, flatter.

"I'm okay," Luke said to Tommy. "I can walk."

"You sure?" Tommy asked.

"Sweet as." Luke forced a quick grin.

Tommy took Luke's arm from around his shoulders but still supported him with a strong grip on his upper arm.

A teenager, about their age, stepped into the corridor in front of them. He looked terrified, his mouth gaping.

Luke instantly recognized the protruding nose and jaw, the high, animal-like ears. It was young Erich Mueller.

Here was their enemy, just a frightened boy, watching the world he knew slowly come to an end.

"Was ist los?" he asked. *"Was ist los?"*

"Amerikanische Soldaten!" Luke said, mimicking Tommy.

Mueller's eyes opened wide in horror, and he disappeared back into his room. Luke stared after him for a second, dumbfounded by the exchange, by the strange twist in time that had him feeling sorry for the child who would grow up to be the man who was currently trying to kill him.

Then Tommy hauled him forward again.

Nobody stopped them. Nobody questioned them.

But the banging on the door behind them stopped, and he suspected that Mueller had managed to talk his way inside.

The corridor into the Werewolf lair was deserted, and they broke into a lurching run, turning off the linking tunnel into the main corridor. Gunfire rattled behind them, and bullets ricocheted off the concrete walls and floor of the tunnel.

"Go," Luke said, and pushed Tommy into the tunnel in front of him. "I'm okay."

They ran a few yards, and Luke could see the odd oval door that led down to the cave of the Vitruvian chamber. Suddenly there was a metallic scraping sound from behind them.

He looked back to see a strange tin can with a long wooden handle bouncing along the floor of the tunnel.

"Grenade!" he shouted. He dived to the side, pushing Tommy through a side door.

The explosion, in the confined space of the tunnel, was ear-shattering, and Luke saw, rather than heard, Tommy mouth the words *Go, go!* as he dragged Luke back to his feet and pushed him through the smoke and smell of cordite, down the corridor.

Then the huge metal door to the lower staircase was in front of them. The handle that had seemed so heavy in the future spun like a feather in their adrenaline-fueled hands.

They slammed the door shut behind them and braced it with a solid length of timber that fitted into two brackets on either side of the door.

Almost immediately, there was a hammering on the other side of the door, but they ignored it and hurried down the long staircase to the cave.

They had reached the bottom and were hauling the second door open when there came another shattering blast from above, and shards of concrete and rock rained down on them from the top of the stairs.

Luke looked up to see the metal door hanging uselessly, limply open, smoke and dust swirling around it.

"Go, go, go!" he yelled, diving through the door after Tommy. He kicked it shut behind him and jammed home the latch just as the thump of an explosion sounded on the other side. Dust billowed around the edges of the door, but it held firmly.

There was a light switch by the door, and he flicked it on, filling the corners of the deep cave with a harsh glare.

The foundations of the metal wall lay in front of them. To the sides were the piles of timber, wire, and boxes of nuts and bolts they had seen earlier. Some empty crates were stacked against the cave wall.

"Come on!" Tommy yelled.

"No! Wait!" Luke shouted. He shuffled over to the wooden crane, holding on to one of the legs for support.

"What?"

Luke tried to calm his breathing and think clearly through the pain from his ribs and leg. "We have to destroy the chamber," he said.

"Let's just get out of here," Tommy said. "Cut some ropes, trap them in 1944."

"That's not enough," Luke said. "We have to destroy it and make sure nobody ever uses it again."

Another explosion sounded behind the metal door, and

more dust blew from around the edges, but it held.

"Let's get back home," Tommy pleaded. "We'll find some explosives and blow the chamber up."

"Where exactly are you going to find explosives?" Luke asked. "And would you know what to do with them if you found them?"

"What, then?"

Luke looked around the cave, and his eyes fell on one of the caches of building materials. "All we need," he said, "is a few nuts and bolts and a bit of wire."

Working through the fear and the pain, they dragged one of the wooden crates of metal bolts beneath the crane. They fed the chain through the carry-handles, then hoisted the crate up as high as it would go.

The crane was on wheels, but there was a locking lever and they had to release each wheel individually before it would move.

There were no more explosions from the metal door, but it shook with a steady hammering.

Luke and Tommy pushed the tall frame of the crane to the center of the cave, using the white chalk cross as a marker.

"I hope this works," Tommy said.

"It will," Luke replied.

The hammering on the door continued, and one of the hinges popped.

"We gotta go," Tommy said.

"Two secs," Luke said.

He grabbed a reel of wire from a pile of building materials. It was light, no more than twelve or fourteen gauge. He twisted one end around the release pin on the block and tackle of the crane, then fed it back toward the door.

The blows of a sledgehammer rained constantly on the other side, and the door shook as he twisted the wire around its handle.

"That's it. Let's go," he said.

The moment the door opened, the release pin would pop and the crate of metal bolts would fall right into the Vitruvian chamber.

They had to be long gone before that happened.

Tommy had pushed a couple of empty crates across the floor below the tripod. He stacked one crate on top of another and then put another crate up against it, to make a stair. They had fallen about half a yard, Luke remembered, so that was how high they needed to be now. The center of the Vitruvian chamber, on the other side of time.

"What if the chamber has stopped working?" Tommy asked. "What do we do if someone has altered the settings?"

"Don't even think about it," Luke said.

Tommy smiled. "You first," he said, helping Luke up onto the first step of the makeshift platform.

Luke looked up at the box of bolts hanging above their heads. "See you next century, bro!" he said.

"You bet, dude," Tommy said.

Luke climbed onto the next level and stood upright.

Instantly, he felt the buzzing and the hair-raising, skin-prickling presence of the chamber. Then the hammering sounds faded into nothingness, as did the bright lights and walls of the cave.

He was back in the chamber, surrounded by the charcoal walls of the rare-earth magnets.

He crawled over to the hatch and looked back to see Tommy right behind him.

"How long have we got?" Luke asked.

"Seconds!" he said. "They're on the last hinge!"

Luke stumbled down through the hatch, falling to the ground, and looked up to see Ms. Sheck's horrified face.

"What happened to you?" she asked.

"Never mind," he yelled. "Just run!"

She didn't run. She stepped toward Luke, bent down, grabbed his arm, and pulled him up over her shoulder in a firefighter's lift. His ribs screamed *fire*, but he gritted his teeth and made no sound.

She ran, and Tommy ran with her, through the diagonal door of the shield wall, to the high concrete staircase leading back to the upper levels.

Tommy slammed the metal door shut behind them.

There were 217 stairs, but Ms. Sheck never once faltered, bounding up with Luke on her shoulder. A strange, fierce shape filled his sight, jumping and bouncing around before his eyes while his exhausted brain tried to make sense of the vision. It snarled, and its eyes burned into him as they put more and more distance between themselves and the impending disaster. They had reached the top of the stairs before Luke realized that he was staring at the tattoo of the roaring lion on her arm.

Tommy slammed open the top door, and they hurried along the corridor.

"What's happening?" Ms. Sheck had little breath to ask.

"I'll tell you soon," Luke said.

In his mind, he could see it all.

The final sledgehammer blow. The door pulling open. The metal wire tightening, then popping the release pin.

The box of metal bolts beginning to fall. Dropping right into the portal between time.

And as it fell, it slipped out of 1944 and into the future, but in the future there was a chamber, made of the strongest, yet most brittle magnets known to man. The most powerful magnetic force ever concentrated in one place.

And the box of heavy iron bolts was about to appear in the middle of it.

The sheer energy, contained in such a small space, was almost impossible to imagine.

Each bolt would accelerate with explosive force, smashing into the brittle fabric of the rare-earth magnets. The chamber would disintegrate, and even as it did so, the flying shards of magnet would attract and repel each other over and over again. It would all happen in an instant.

Even as he thought that, the ground heaved beneath their feet and they were thrown down.

The metal door behind them was blown off its hinges like a sliver of tinfoil, rock and dust billowing into the tunnels behind them.

Then, almost immediately, came an implosion, the dust and smoke sucked back down into the depths of the tunnels, rushing back to fill the vacuum that had been created.

For a moment, all the air disappeared and they gasped for

breath, before the pressure slowly began to return to normal.

It was over.

The chamber was gone.

The book, *Leonardo's River*, was destroyed along with it.

Hitler would lose the war, and the world, for good or bad, would be the same as it always had been.

Mueller himself would be trapped. An old man trapped in the wrong time.

He might try to tell people of the future, but they would just think him crazy.

A crazy old man.

Ms. Sheck was first to her feet and extended a hand down to Tommy and then Luke.

Luke took it and stood, brushing dust and rock particles from his clothes.

"Where's Gerda?" he asked.

"She left," Ms. Sheck said. "I don't know where she went."

There was a long period of silence; then she asked, "Are you going to tell me what happened?"

Despite the shock and the pain, or perhaps because of it, Luke laughed. "Can it be our new project, instead of *The Last of the Mohicans*?"

Ms. Sheck smiled.

EPILOGUE

Tommy and I told Ms. Sheck most of what happened, but we also swore each other to secrecy.

The ability to change the past and steal knowledge from the future. Was there anybody on earth who would not abuse that power?

Leonardo was right. If it came to light, then someone, somewhere, would misuse it.

Leonardo's drawings had been destroyed by Benfer, and Benfer's book, and the chamber itself, had been lost in the explosion at the bunker.

So that, pretty much, was that.

Almost.

Somehow, even though I knew the risks, I could not bring myself to completely destroy this centuries-old knowledge. The most amazing discovery of Leonardo da Vinci.

I justified it to myself by thinking that maybe one day there would be some terrible catastrophe, like a nuclear war, and the Vitruvian chamber could be rebuilt to save the world from disaster. That maybe in the future, people would learn to live in harmony and to use the knowledge responsibly.

But I knew that really I was just making excuses.

Like Benfer, I couldn't bring myself to wipe the knowledge completely from the face of the earth.

And the plans did still exist, of course.

In the strange and fickle memory of a fifteen-year-old boy.

I knew I couldn't rely on that memory forever. I had to record Leonardo's calculations somewhere.

But where?

How could I hide this information so thoroughly, so completely, that it could never be found, and yet at the same time, it was not forever lost?

A code.

I needed a code that would be impossible to break, protected by a key that was infinite.

It took me a year. Six months to create the code, and another six months to encode the numbers and the diagrams.

And where to store the code? There was only one place, of course. Woven into words, secreted into sentences, pasted into paragraphs, concealed into chapters, buried in a book.

Hidden in plain sight.

I went to Dad's computer and laid out the sheets of encoded data beside me on the desk. Then I typed the first words of my novel slowly, knowing that everyone who read these words would regard it as just a story. Fiction. No one would ever believe that it was true.

"This is not the most boring book in the world," I wrote. *"This is a book* about *the most boring book in the world."* I considered that for a moment, then replaced the period with a comma and added: *"which is a different book altogether."*

CONGRATULATIONS

The following people won the grand prize in my school competitions and have all had a character named after them in this book:

DARCY BENFER
Brisbane Boys' College, Queensland, Australia

BRYAN BROWN
Vista Del Valle School, California, United States

GLENN DINNING
Mount Tarampa State School, Queensland, Australia

AARON FAYERS
Lincoln Heights School, New Zealand

JACOB ISHERWOOD
Kimberley College, Queensland, Australia

MR. KERR
Masterton Intermediate School, New Zealand

PHILIPP KHODIER
St. Patrick's College Strathfield, NSW, Australia

BEN PICKERING
Point View School, New Zealand

JENNIFER SEDDON
Tinopai Primary School, New Zealand

CLAUDIA SMITH
St. Joseph's School, New Zealand

ALSO:
Luke McKay, Laetitia Sheck,
Heath Thompson, Tom Wundheiler

THANKS

Chris Doyle
strength coach, University of Iowa Hawkeyes

Kristi Bontrager
public relations coordinator,
University of Iowa Libraries

Christopher Merrill
International Writing Program (IWP), University
of Iowa, for his firsthand account of the floods

The IWP team:
Hugh Ferrer
Joe Tiefenthaler
Melissa Schiek
Kiki Petrosino
Kelly Bedeian
Nataša Ďurovičová
Peter and Mary Nazareth
Kecia Lynn

Don't miss Brian Falkner's next action thriller—

THE
ASSAULT

HUMANITY IS LOSING . . .

the war against its alien invaders. Earth has been almost entirely conquered, with the Americas as the last free territories still under human rule. This could be humanity's last chance to strike back.

A team of six has been chosen . . .

to infiltrate the enemy's headquarters in the heart of the Australian Outback. The six teens have been modified to look like aliens. They have spent years mastering alien culture so that they can talk, act—even think—like their enemies. But from the start, the recon mission goes terribly wrong. It's only when they are close to discovering the shocking truth of the aliens' plans that the team is forced to ask:

Is there a traitor among them?